DAVY
and the
GOBLIN

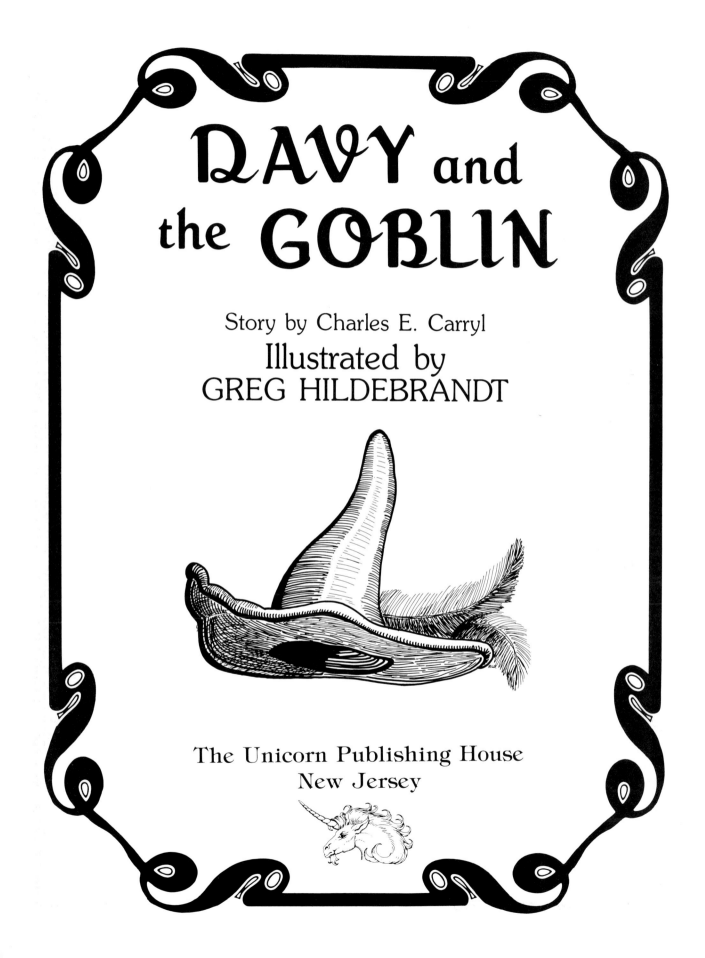

DAVY and the GOBLIN

Story by Charles E. Carryl

Illustrated by
GREG HILDEBRANDT

The Unicorn Publishing House
New Jersey

Designed and edited by Jean L. Scrocco
Associate Juvenile Editor: Heidi K.L. Corso
Printed in Singapore by Singapore National Printers Ltd through Palace Press
Typography by Straight Creek Company, Denver, CO
Reproduction Photography by The Color Wheel, New York, NY

• • • • •

Cover and interior graphics by R.L. Rebach

• • • • •

Distributed in Canada by Doubleday Canada, Ltd., Toronto, ON M5B 1Y3, Canada

• • • • •

Special thanks to the entire Unicorn staff.

• • • • •

Printing History 15 14 13 12 11 10 9 8 7 6 5 4 3 2 1

• • • • •

Library of Congress Cataloging-in-Publication Data

Carryl, Charles E. (Charles Edward), 1841-1920.
Davy and the goblin.

Summary: A little boy, who believes that fairies and goblins are strictly creatures of fantasy, gets taken on a "Believing Voyage" by a hobgoblin.
[1. Fantasy] I. Hildebrandt, Greg, ill. II. Title.
PZ7.C2373Dav 1988 [Fic] 88-10758
ISBN 0-88101-083-9

Additional Classic and Contemporary Editions
Richly Illustrated in
This Unicorn Heirloom Collection:

PHANTOM OF THE OPERA
AESOP'S FABLES
POLLYANNA
TWENTY THOUSAND LEAGUES UNDER THE SEAS
PETER PAN
ANTIQUE FAIRY TALES
PINOCCHIO
POE
THE WIZARD OF OZ
DRACULA
HEIDI
FROM TOLKIEN TO OZ
PETER COTTONTAIL'S SURPRISE
A CHRISTMAS TREASURY
TREASURES OF CHANUKAH

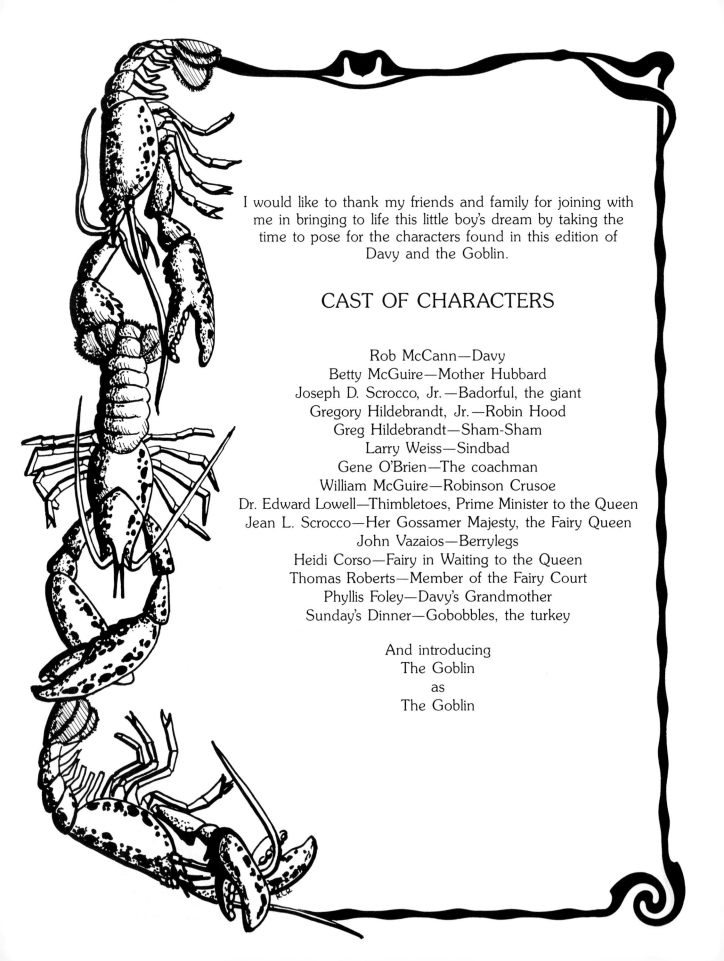

I would like to thank my friends and family for joining with me in bringing to life this little boy's dream by taking the time to pose for the characters found in this edition of Davy and the Goblin.

CAST OF CHARACTERS

Rob McCann—Davy
Betty McGuire—Mother Hubbard
Joseph D. Scrocco, Jr.—Badorful, the giant
Gregory Hildebrandt, Jr.—Robin Hood
Greg Hildebrandt—Sham-Sham
Larry Weiss—Sindbad
Gene O'Brien—The coachman
William McGuire—Robinson Crusoe
Dr. Edward Lowell—Thimbletoes, Prime Minister to the Queen
Jean L. Scrocco—Her Gossamer Majesty, the Fairy Queen
John Vazaios—Berrylegs
Heidi Corso—Fairy in Waiting to the Queen
Thomas Roberts—Member of the Fairy Court
Phyllis Foley—Davy's Grandmother
Sunday's Dinner—Gobobbles, the turkey

And introducing
The Goblin
as
The Goblin

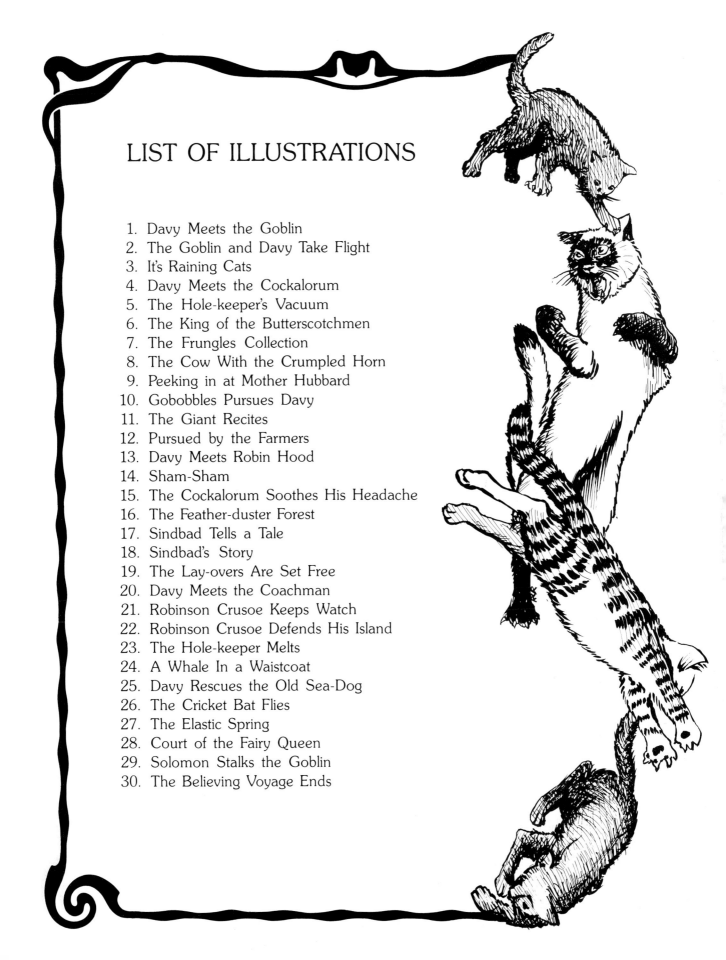

LIST OF ILLUSTRATIONS

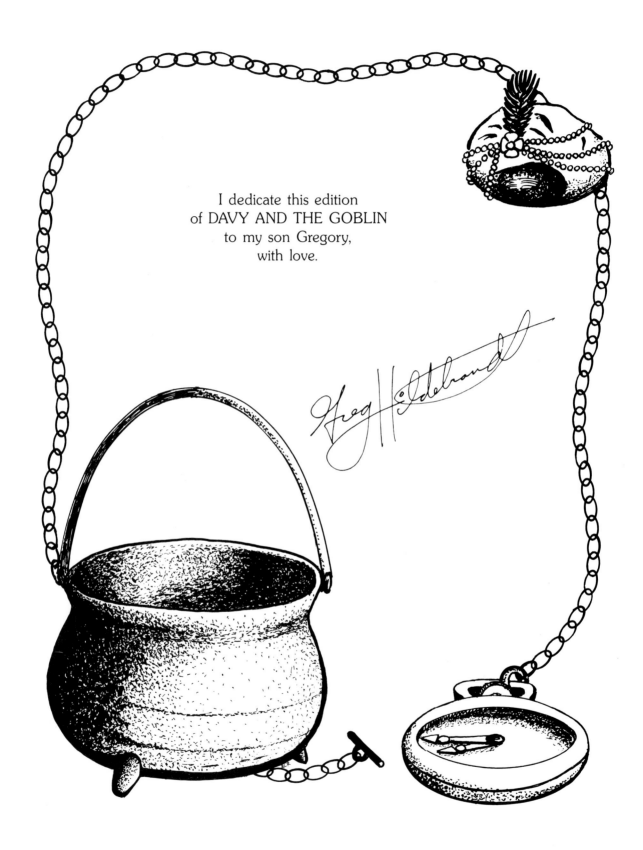

I dedicate this edition
of DAVY AND THE GOBLIN
to my son Gregory,
with love.

Greg Hildebrandt

LIST OF CHAPTERS

CHAPTER I

HOW THE GOBLIN CAME

It happened one Christmas eve, when Davy was about eight years old, and this is the way it came about.

That particular Christmas eve was a snowy one and a blowy one, and one generally to be remembered. In the city, where Davy lived, the storm played all manner of pranks, swooping down upon unwary old gentlemen and turning their umbrellas wrong side out, and sometimes blowing their hats quite out of sight; as for the old ladies who chanced to be out-of-doors, the wind came upon them suddenly from around corners and blew the snow into their faces and twisted their petticoats about their ankles, and even whirled the old ladies themselves about in a very painful way. And in the country, where Davy had come to pass Christmas with his dear old grandmother, things were not much better; but here people were very wise about the weather, and stayed in-doors, huddled around great blazing wood fires; and the storm, finding no live game, buried up the roads and the fences, and such small fry of houses as could readily be put out of sight, and howled and roared over the fields and through the trees in a fashion not to be forgotten.

Davy, being of the opinion that a snow-storm was a thing not be wasted, had been out with his sled, trying to have a little fun with the weather; but presently, discovering that this particular storm was not friendly to little boys, he had retreated into the house, and having put his hat and his high shoes and his mittens by the kitchen fire to dry, he began to find his time hang heavily on his hands. He had wandered idly all over the house, and had tried how cold his nose could be made by holding it against the windowpanes, and, I am sorry to say, had even been sliding down the balusters and teasing the cat; and at last, as evening was coming on, had curled himself up in the big easy-chair facing the fire, and had begun to read once more about the marvelous things that happened to little Alice in Wonderland. Then, as it grew darker, he laid aside the book and sat watching the blazing logs and listening to the solemn ticking of the high Dutch clock against the wall.

Then there stole in at the door a delicious odor of dinner cooking downstairs,—an odor so promising as to roast chickens and baked potatoes and gravy and pie as to make any little boy's mouth water; and presently Davy began softly telling himself what he would choose for his dinner. He had quite finished fancying the first part of his feast, and was just coming, in his mind, to an extra large slice of apple-pie well browned (staring meanwhile very hard at one of the brass knobs of the andirons to keep his thoughts from wandering), when he suddenly discovered a little man perched upon that identical knob, and smiling at him with all his might.

The little man was a very curious-looking person indeed. He was only about a foot high, but his head was as big as a cocoanut, and he had great, bulging eyes, like a frog, and a ridiculous turned-up nose. His legs were as slender as spindles, and he had long pointed toes to his shoes, or rather to his stockings, or, for that matter, to his trousers—for they were all of a piece—and bright scarlet in color, as were also his little coat and his high-pointed hat and a queer little cloak that hung over his shoulder. His mouth was so wide that when he smiled it seemed to go quite behind his ears, and there was no way of knowing where the smile ended, except by looking at it from behind, which Davy couldn't do, as yet, without getting into the fire.

Now, there's no use in denying that Davy was frightened. The fact is, he was frightened almost out of his wits, particularly when he saw that the little man, still smiling furiously, was carefully picking the hottest and reddest embers out of the fire, and, after cracking them like nuts with his teeth, eating them with great relish. Davy watched this alarming meal, expecting every moment to see the little man burst into a blaze and disappear; but he finished his coals in safety, and then, nodding cheerfully at Davy, said:—

"I know you!"

"Do you?" said Davy, faintly.

"Oh, yes!" said the little man. "I know you perfectly well. You are the little boy who doesn't believe in fairies, nor in giants, nor in goblins, nor in anything the story-books tell you."

Now the truth was that Davy, having never met any giants when he was out walking, nor seen any fairies peeping out of the bushes in the garden, nor found any goblins sitting on the bedposts about the house, had come to believe that all these kinds of people were purely imaginary beings, so that now he could do nothing but stare at the little man in a shamefaced sort of way and wonder what was coming next.

"Now, all that," said the little man, shaking his finger at him in a reproving way,— "all that is very foolish and very wrong. I'm a goblin myself—a hobgoblin—and I've come to take you on a Believing Voyage."

"Oh, if you please, I can't go!" cried Davy, in great alarm at this proposal; "I can't, indeed. I haven't permission."

"Rubbish!" said the Goblin. "Ask the Colonel."

Now the Colonel was nothing more nor less than a silly-looking little man, made of lead, that stood on the mantel-shelf holding a clock in his arms. The clock never went, but, for that matter, the Colonel never went either, for he had been standing stock-still for years, and it seemed perfectly ridiculous to ask *him* anything about going anywhere, so Davy felt quite safe in looking up at him and asking permission to go on the Believing Voyage. To his dismay the Colonel nodded his head, and cried out, in a little, cracked voice:—

"Why, certainly!"

At this the Goblin jumped down off the knob of the andiron, and skipping briskly across the room to the big Dutch clock, rapped sharply on the front of the case with his knuckles, when, to Davy's amazement, the great thing fell over on its face upon the floor as softly as if it had been a feather-bed. Davy now saw that, instead of being full of weights and brass wheels and curious works, as he had always supposed, the clock was really a sort of boat, with a wide seat at each end; but, before he had time to make any further discoveries, the Goblin, who had vanished for a moment, suddenly reappeared, carrying two large sponge-cakes in his arms. Now, Davy was perfectly sure that he had seen his grandmother putting those very sponge-cakes into the oven to bake, but before he could utter a word of remonstrance the Goblin clapped one into each seat, and scrambling into the clock sat down upon the smaller one, merely remarking:—

"They make prime cushions, you know, and we can eat 'em afterwards."

For a moment Davy had a wild idea of rushing out of the room and calling for help; but the Goblin seemed so pleased with the arrangements he had made, and, moreover, was smiling so good-naturedly, that the little boy thought better of it, and, after a moment's hesitation, climbed into the clock and took his seat upon the other cake. It was as warm and springy, and smelt as deliciously, as a morning in May. Then there was a whizzing sound, like a lot of wheels spinning around, and the clock rose from the floor and made a great swoop toward the window.

"I'll steer," shouted the Goblin, "and do you look out sharp for cats and dogs," and Davy had just time to notice that the Colonel was hastily scrambling down from the mantel-shelf with his beloved timepiece in his arms, when they, seated in the long Dutch clock, dashed through the window and out into the night.

CHAPTER II

THE BEGINNING OF THE BELIEVING VOYAGE

he first thought that came into Davy's mind when he found himself out-of-doors was that he had started off on his journey without his hat, and he was therefore exceedingly pleased to find that it had stopped snowing and that the air was quite still and delightfully balmy and soft. The moon was shining brightly, and as he looked back at the house he was surprised to see that the window through which they had come, and which he was quite sure had always been a straight-up-and-down, old-fashioned window, was now a round affair, with flaps running to a point in the centre, like the holes the harlequin jumps through in the pantomime.

"How did that window ever get changed into a round hole?" he asked the Goblin, pointing to it in great astonishment.

"Oh," said the Goblin, carelessly, "that's one of the circular circumstances that happen on a Believing Voyage. It's nothing to what you'll see before we come back again. Ah!" he added, "there comes the Colonel!"

Sure enough, at this moment the Colonel's head appeared through the flaps. The clock was still in his arms, and he seemed to be having a great deal of trouble in getting it through, and his head kept coming into view and then disappearing again behind the flaps in so ridiculous a manner that Davy shouted with laughter, and the Goblin smiled harder than ever. Suddenly the poor little man made a desperate plunge, and had almost made his way out when the flaps shut to with a loud snap and caught him about the waist. In his efforts to free himself he dropped his clock to the ground outside, when it burst with a loud explosion, and the house instantly disappeared.

This was so unexpected, and seemed so serious a matter, that Davy was much distressed, wondering what had become of his dear old grandmother, and Mrs. Frump, the cook, and Mary Farina, the housemaid, and Solomon, the cat. However, before he had time to make any inquiries of the Goblin, his grandmother came dropping down through the air in her rocking chair. She was quietly knitting, and her chair was gently rocking as she went by. Next came Mrs. Frump, with her apron quite full of kettles and pots, and then Mary Farina, sitting on a step-ladder with the coal-scuttle in her lap. Solomon was nowhere to be seen. Davy, looking over the side of the clock, saw them disappear, one after the other, in a large tree on the lawn, and the Goblin informed him that they had fallen into the kitchen of a witch-hazel tree, and would be well taken care of. Indeed, as the clock sailed over the tree, Davy saw that the trunk of it was hollow, and that a bright light was shining far underground; and, to make the matter quite sure, a smell of cooking was coming up through the hole. On one of the topmost boughs of the tree was a nest with two sparrows in it, and he was much astonished at discovering that they were lying side by side, fast asleep, with one of his mittens spread over them for a coverlet. I am sorry to say that Davy knew perfectly well where the other mitten was, and was ashamed to say anything about it.

"I suppose my shoes are somewhere about," he said, sadly. "Perhaps the squirrels are filling them with nuts."

"You're quite right," replied the Goblin, cheerfully; "and there's a rabbit over by the hedge putting dried leaves into your hat. I rather fancy he's about moving into it for the winter."

Davy was about to complain against such liberties being taken with his property, when the clock began rolling over in the air, and he had just time to grasp the sides of it to keep himself from falling out.

"Don't be afraid!" cried the Goblin, "she's only rolling a little;" and, as he said this, the clock steadied itself and sailed serenely away past the spire of the village church and off over the fields.

Davy now noticed that the Goblin was glowing with a bright, rosy light, as though a number of candles were burning in his stomach and shining out through his scarlet clothes.

"That's the coals he had for his supper," thought Davy; but, as the Goblin continued to smile complacently and seemed to be feeling quite comfortable, he did not venture to ask any questions, and went on with his thoughts. "I suppose he'll soon have smoke coming out of his nose, as if he were a stove. If it were a cold night I'd ask him to come and sit in my lap. I think he must be as warm as a piece of toast;" and the little boy was laughing softly to himself over this conceit, when the Goblin, who had been staring intently at the sky, suddenly ducked his head, and cried "Squalls!" and the next moment the air was filled with cats falling in a perfect shower from the sky.

They were of all sizes and colors, —big cats, little cats, black cats, white cats, gray cats, yellow, spotted and brindle cats, and at least a dozen of them fell sprawling into the clock. Among them, to Davy's dismay, was Solomon, with the other mitten drawn over his head and the thumb sticking straight up like a horn. This gave him a very extraordinary appearance, and the other cats evidently regarded him with the gravest distrust as they clustered together at Davy's end of the clock, leaving Solomon standing quite alone, and complaining in a muffled voice as he tugged frantically at the mitten.

"Don't scold so much!" said the Goblin, impatiently.

Now, Davy would never have teased Solomon if he had had the slightest idea that cats could talk, and he was dreadfully mortified when Solomon cried out excitedly, "Scold! I should think I had enough to scold about to-day! I've had bits of worsted tied on to my tail, and I've had some milk with pepper in it, and I've had pill-boxes stuck on to my feet, so that I fell heels over head downstairs—let alone having this nightcap on!"

All this was certainly enough to scold about; but what else Solomon had to complain of will never be known, for, at this moment, an old tabby cat screamed out, "Barkers!" and all the cats sprang over the side of the clock, and disappeared, with Solomon bringing up the rear, like a little unicorn.

"I think it sounds very ridiculous for a cat to talk in that way," said Davy, uneasily.

"Yes; but it sounds very true, for all that," said the Goblin, gravely.

"But it was such fun, you know," said Davy, feeling that he was blushing violently.

"Oh, I dare say! Fun for *you*," said the Goblin, sarcastically. "Jolligong! Here come the Barkers!" he added, and, as he said this, a shower of little blue woolly balls came tumbling into the clock. To Davy's alarm they proved to be alive, and immediately began scrambling about in all directions, and yelping so ferociously that he climbed up on his cake in dismay, while the Goblin, hastily pulling a large magnifying-glass out of his hat, began attentively examining these strange visitors.

"Bless me!" cried the Goblin, turning very pale, "they're sky-terriers. The dog-star must have turned upside-down."

"What shall we do?" said Davy, feeling that this was a very bad state of affairs.

"The first thing to do," said the Goblin, "is to get away from these fellows before the solar sisters come after them. Here, jump into my hat."

So many wonderful things had happened already that this seemed to Davy quite a natural and proper thing to do, and as the Goblin had already seated himself upon the brim, he took his place opposite to him without hesitation. As they sailed away from the clock it quietly rolled over once, spilling out the sponge-cakes and all the little dogs, and was then wafted off, gently rocking from side to side as it went.

Davy was much surprised at finding that the hat was as large as a clothes-hamper, with plenty of room for him to swing his legs about in the crown. It proved, however, to be a very unpleasant thing to travel in. It spun around like a top as it sailed through the air, until Davy began to feel uncomfortably dizzy, and the Goblin himself seemed to be far from well. He had stopped smiling, and the rosy light had all faded away, as though the candles inside of him had gone out. His clothes, too, had changed from bright scarlet to a dull ashen color, and he sat stupidly upon the brim of the hat as if he were going to sleep.

"If he goes to sleep he will certainly fall overboard," thought Davy; and, with a view to rousing the Goblin, he ventured to remark, "I had no idea your hat was so big."

"I can make it any size I please, from a thimble to a sentry-box," said the Goblin. "And, speaking of sentry-boxes"—here he stopped and looked more stupid than ever.

"I verily believe he's absent-minded," said Davy to himself.

"I'm worse than that," said the Goblin, as if Davy had spoken aloud. "I'm absent-bodied;" and with these words he fell out of the hat and instantly disappeared. Davy peered anxiously over the edge of the brim; but the Goblin was nowhere to be seen, and the little boy found himself quite alone.

Strange-looking birds now began to swoop up and chuckle at him, and others flew around him, as the hat spun along through the air, gravely staring him in the face for a while, and then sailed away, sadly bleating like sheep. Then a great creature, with rumpled feathers, perched upon the brim of the hat where the Goblin had been sitting, and, after solemnly gazing at him for a few moments, softly murmured, "I'm a Cockalorum," and flew heavily away. All this was very sad and distressing, and Davy was mournfully wondering what would happen to him next, when it suddenly struck him that his legs were feeling very cold, and, looking down at them, he discovered, to his great alarm, that the crown of the Goblin's hat had entirely disappeared, leaving nothing but the brim, upon which he was sitting. He hurriedly examined this, and found the hat was really nothing but an enormous skein of wool, which was rapidly unwinding as it spun along. Indeed, the brim was disappearing at such a rate that he had hardly made this alarming discovery before the end of the skein was whisked away, and he found himself falling through the air.

He was on the point of screaming out in his terror, when he discovered that he was falling very slowly and gently swaying from side to side, like a toy-balloon. The next moment he struck something hard, which gave way with a sound like breaking glass and let him through, and he had just time to notice that the air had suddenly become deliciously scented with vanilla, when he fell crashing into the branches of a large tree.

CHAPTER III

IN THE SUGAR-PLUM GARDEN

he bough upon which Davy had fallen bent far down with his weight, then sprang back, then bent again, and in this way fell into a sort of delightful up-and-down dipping motion, which he found very soothing and agreeable. Indeed, he was so pleased and comforted at finding himself near the ground once more that he lay back in a crotch between two branches, enjoying the rocking of the bough, and lazily wondering what had become of the Goblin, and whether this was the end of the Believing Voyage, and a great many other things, until he chanced to wonder where he was. Then he sat up on the branch in great astonishment, for he saw that the tree was in full leaf and loaded with plums, and it flashed across his mind that the winter had disappeared very suddenly, and that he had fallen into a place where it was broad daylight.

The plum-tree was the most beautiful and wonderful thing he had ever seen, for the leaves were perfectly white, and the plums, which looked extremely delicious, were of every imaginable color.

Now, it immediately occurred to Davy that he had never in his whole life had all the plums he wanted at any one time. Here was a rare chance for a feast, and he carefully selected the largest and most luscious-looking plum he could find, to begin with. To his disappointment it proved to be quite hard, and as solid and heavy as a stone. He was looking at it in great perplexity, and punching it with his thumbs in the hope of finding a soft place in it, when he heard a rustling sound among the leaves, and, looking up, he saw the Cockalorum perched upon the bough beside him. He was gazing sadly at the plum, and his feathers were more rumpled than ever. Presently he gave a long sigh and said, in his low, murmuring voice, "Perhaps it's a sugar-plum," and then flew clumsily away as before.

"Perhaps it is!" exclaimed Davy, joyfully, taking a great bite of the plum. To his surprise and disgust he found his mouth full of very bad-tasting soap, and at the same moment the white leaves of the plum-tree suddenly turned over and showed the words "APRIL FOOL" printed very distinctly on their under sides. To make the matter worse, the Cockalorum came back and flew slowly around the branches, laughing softly to himself with a sort of a chuckling sound, until Davy, almost crying with disappointment and mortification, scrambled down from the tree to the ground.

He found himself in a large garden planted with plum-trees, like the one he had fallen into, and with walks winding about among them in every direction. These walks were beautifully paved with sugar-almonds and bordered by long rows of many-colored motto-papers neatly planted in the ground. He was too much distressed, however, by what had happened in the plum-tree to be interested or pleased with this discovery, and was about walking away, along one of the paths, in the hope of finding his way out of the garden, when he suddenly caught sight of a small figure standing a little distance from him.

He was the strangest-looking creature Davy had ever seen, not even excepting the Goblin. In the first place he was as flat as a pancake, and about as thick as one; and, in the second place, he was so transparent that Davy could see through his head and his arms and his legs almost as clearly as though he had been made of glass. This was so surprising in itself that when Davy presently discovered that he was made of beautiful, clear lemon candy, it seemed the most natural thing in the world, as explaining his transparency. He was neatly dressed in a sort of tunic of writing-paper, with a cocked hat of the same material, and he had under his arm a large book, with the words "HOLE-KEEPER'S VACUUM" printed on the cover. This curious-looking creature was standing before an extremely high wall, with his back to Davy, intently watching a large hole in the wall about a foot from the ground. There was nothing extraordinary about the appearance of the hole (except that the lower edge of it was curiously tied in a large bow-knot, like a cravat); but Davy watched it carefully for a few moments, thinking that perhaps something marvellous would come out of it. Nothing appeared, however, and Davy, walking up close behind the candy man, said very politely, "If you please, sir, I dropped in here"—

Before he could finish the sentence the Hole-keeper said snappishly, "Well, drop out again—quick!"

"But," pleaded Davy, "you can't drop out of a place, you know, unless the place should happen to turn upside down."

"I *don't* know anything about it," replied the Hole-keeper, without moving. "I never saw anything drop—except once. Then I saw a gum-drop. Are you a gum?" he added, suddenly turning around and staring at Davy.

"Of course I'm not," said Davy, indignantly. "If you'll only listen to me, you'll understand exactly how it happened."

"Well, go on," said the Hole-keeper, impatiently, "and don't be tiresome."

"I fell down ever so far," said Davy, beginning his story over again, "and at last I broke through something"—

"That was the skylight!" shrieked the Hole-keeper, dashing his book upon the ground in a fury. "That was the barley-sugar skylight, and I shall certainly be boiled!"

This was such a shocking idea that Davy stood speechless, staring at the Hole-keeper, who rushed to and fro in a convulsion of distress.

"Now, see here," said the Hole-keeper, at length, coming up to him and speaking in a low, trembling voice. "This must be a private secret between us. Do you solemsy promilse?"

"I prolemse," said Davy, earnestly. This wasn't at all what he meant to say, and it sounded very ridiculous; but somehow the words *wouldn't* come straight. The Hole-keeper, however, seemed perfectly satisfied, and, picking up his book, said, "Well, just wait till I can't find your name," and began hurriedly turning over the leaves.

Davy saw, to his astonishment, that there was nothing whatever in the book, all the leaves being perfectly blank, and he couldn't help saying, rather contemptuously:—

"How do you expect to find my name in *that* book? There's nothing in it."

"Ah! that's just it, you see," said the Hole-keeper, exultingly; "I look in it for the names that ought to be out of it. It's the completest system that *ever* was invented. Oh! here you aren't!" he added, staring with great satisfaction at one of the blank pages. "Your name is Rupsy Frimbles."

"It's nothing of the sort," said Davy, indignantly.

"Tut! Tut!" said the Hole-keeper. "Don't stop to contradict or you'll be too late;" and Davy felt himself gently lifted off his feet and pushed head-foremost into the hole. It was quite dark and rather sticky, and smelt strongly of burnt sugar, and Davy had a most unpleasant time of it crawling through on his hands and knees. To add to his distress, when he came out at the further end, instead of being, as he had hoped, in the open country, he found himself in a large room, with a lofty ceiling, through which a brilliant light was mysteriously shining. The floor was of tin, and greased to such a slippery degree that Davy could hardly keep his feet, and against the walls on all sides were ranged long rows of little tin chairs glistening like silver in the dazzling light.

The only person in the room was a little man, something like the Hole-keeper in appearance, but denser and darker in the way of complexion, and dressed in a brown paper tunic and cocked hat.

This little creature was carrying a pail, and apparently varnishing the chairs with a little swab as he moved swiftly about the room; and, as he came nearer, Davy determined to speak to him.

"If you please," he began.

The little man jumped back apparently in the greatest alarm, and, after a startled

look at Davy, shuffled rapidly away and disappeared through a door at the further end of the room. The next moment a confused sound of harsh voices came through the door, and the little man reappeared, followed by a perfect swarm of creatures so exactly like himself that it seemed to Davy as if a thousand of him had come back. At this moment a voice called out, "Bring Frungles this way;" and the crowd gathered around him and began to rudely hustle him across the room.

"That's not my name!" cried Davy, struggling desperately to free himself. "It isn't even the name I came in with!"

"Tut! Tut!" said a trembling voice near him; and Davy caught sight of the Hole-keeper, also struggling in the midst of the crowd, with his great book hugged tightly to his breast.

"What does it all mean?" said Davy, anxiously.

"It means that we are to be taken before the king," said the Hole-keeper, in an agitated voice. "Don't say a word until you are spoken to, and then keep perfectly still;" and the next moment they were dragged up to a low platform, where the king was sitting on a gorgeous tin throne. He was precisely like the rest of the creatures, except that he was a little larger, and wore a blue paper coat and a sparkling tin crown, and held in his hand a long white wand, with red lines running screw-wise around it, like a barber's pole. He stared at Davy and the Hole-keeper for a moment, and then called out, "Are the chairs buttered?"

"They are!" shouted the crowd, like one man.

"Then sit down!" roared the king.

The crowd shuffled off in all directions, and then engaged in a confused struggle for the chairs. They fought desperately for a few moments, tearing each others' shirts, and screaming out hoarse little squawks of pain, while the king thumped furiously with his wand, and the Hole-keeper trembled like a leaf. At last all were seated and the hub-bub ceased, and the king, frowning savagely at the Hole-keeper, exclaimed, in a terrible voice, "Who broke the barley-sugar skylight?"

The Hole-keeper began fumbling at the leaves of his book in great agitation, when the king, pointing at him with his wand, roared furiously: "Boil *him*, at all events!"

"Tut! Tut! your majesty," began the Hole-keeper, confusedly, with his stiff little tunic fairly rustling with fright; but before he could utter another word he was rushed upon and dragged away, screaming with terror.

"Don't you go with them!" shouted Davy, made really desperate by the Hole-keeper's danger. "They're nothing but a lot of molasses candy!"

At this the king gave a frightful shriek, and, aiming a furious blow at Davy with his wand, rolled off the platform into the midst of the struggling crowd. The wand broke into a hundred pieces, and the air was instantly filled with a choking odor of peppermint; then everything was wrapped in darkness, and Davy felt himself being whirled

along, heels over head, through the air. Then there came a confused sound of bells and voices, and he found himself running rapidly down a long street with the Goblin at his side.

CHAPTER IV

THE BUTTERSCOTCHMEN

ells were pealing and tolling in all directions, and the air was filled with the sound of distant shouts and cries.

"What were they?" asked Davy, breathlessly.

"Butterscotchmen," said the Goblin. "You see, they always butter their chairs so that they won't stick fast when they sit down."

"And what makes you that color?" said Davy, suddenly noticing that the Goblin had changed his color to a beautiful blue.

"Trouble and worry," said the Goblin. "I always get blue when the Butterscotchmen are after me."

"Are they coming after us now?" inquired Davy, in great alarm.

"Of course they are," said the Goblin. "But the best of it is, they can't run till they get warm, and they can't get warm without running, you see. But the worst of it is that *we* can't stop without sticking fast," he added, anxiously. "We must keep it up until we get to the Amuserum."

"What's that?" said Davy.

"It's a place they have to amuse themselves with," said the Goblin, — "curiosities, and all that sort of thing, you know. By the way, how much money have you? We have to pay to get in."

Davy began to feel in his pockets (which is a very difficult thing to do when you're running fast), and found, to his astonishment, that they were completely filled with a most extraordinary lot of rubbish. First he pulled out what seemed to be an iron ball; but it proved to be a hardboiled egg, without the shell, stuck full of small tacks. Then came two slices of toast, firmly tied together with a green cord. Then came a curious little glass jar, filled with large flies. As Davy took this out of his pocket, the cork came out with a loud "pop!" and the flies flew away in all directions. Then came, one after another, a tart filled with gravel, two chicken-bones, a bird's nest with some pieces of brown soap in it, some mustard in a pill-box, and a cake of beeswax stuck full of caraway seeds. Davy remembered afterward that, as he threw these things away, they arranged themselves in a long row on the curb-stone of the street. The Goblin looked on with great interest as Davy fished them up out of his pockets, and finally said, enviously, "That's a splendid collection; where did they all come from?"

"I'm sure *I* don't know," said Davy, in great bewilderment.

"And I'm sure *I* don't know," repeated the Goblin. "What else is there?"

Davy felt about in his pockets again, and found what seemed to be a piece of money. On taking it out, however, he was mortified to find that it was nothing but an old button; but the Goblin exclaimed, in a tone of great satisfaction, "Ah! hold on to that!" and ran on faster than ever.

The sound of the distant voices had grown fainter and fainter still, and Davy was just hoping that their long run was almost over, when the street came abruptly to an end at a brick wall, over the top of which he could see the branches of trees. There was a small round hole in the wall, with the words "PAY HERE" printed above it, and the Goblin whispered to Davy to hand in the button through this hole. Davy did so, feeling very much ashamed of himself, when, to his surprise, instead of receiving tickets in return, he heard a loud exclamation behind the wall, followed by a confused sound of scuffling, and the hole suddenly disappeared. The next moment a little bell tinkled, and the wall rose slowly before them like a curtain, carrying the trees with it apparently, and he and the Goblin were left standing in a large open space paved with stone.

Davy was exceedingly alarmed at seeing a dense mass of Butterscotchmen in the centre of the square, pushing and crowding one another in a very quarrelsome manner, and chattering like a flock of magpies, and he was just about to propose a hasty retreat, when a figure came hurrying through the square, carrying on a pole a large placard, bearing the words:—

> JUST RECEIVED!
> THE GREAT FRUNGLES THING!
> ON EXHIBITION IN THE PLUM-GARDEN!

At the sight of these words the mob set up a terrific shout, and began streaming out of the square after the polebearer, like a flock of sheep, jostling and shoving one another as they went, and leaving Davy and the Goblin quite alone.

"I verily believe they're gone to look at my button," cried Davy, beginning to laugh, in spite of his fears. "They called *me* Frungles, you know."

"That's rather a nice name," said the Goblin, who had begun smiling again. "It's better than Snubgraddle, at all events. Let's have a look at the curiosities;" and here he walked boldly into the centre of the square.

Davy followed close at his heels, and found, to his astonishment and disappointment, that the curiosities were simply the things that he had fished out of his pockets but a few minutes before, placed on little pedestals and carefully protected by transparent sugar shades. He was on the point of laughing outright at this ridiculous exhibition, when he saw that the Goblin had taken a large telescope out of his pocket, and was examining the different objects with the closest attention, and muttering to himself, "Wonderful! wonderful!" as if he had never seen anything like them before.

"Pooh!" said Davy contemptuously; "the only wonderful thing about them is, how they ever came *here.*"

At this remark the Goblin turned his telescope toward Davy, and uttered a faint cry of surprise; and Davy, peering anxiously through the large end, saw him suddenly shrink to the size of a small beetle, and then disappear altogether. Davy hastily reached out with his hands to grasp the telescope, and found himself staring through a round glass window into a farm-yard, where a red Cow stood gazing up at him.

• CHAPTER V •

JACK AND THE BEAN-STALK'S FARM

t was quite an ordinary-looking farm-yard and quite an ordinary-looking Cow, but she stared so earnestly up at Davy that he felt positively certain she had something to say to him. "Every creature I meet *does* have something to say," he thought, as he felt about for the window-fastening, "and I should really like to hear a Cow"—and just at this moment the window suddenly flew open, and he pitched head-foremost, out upon a pile of hay in the farm-yard, and rolled from it off upon the ground. As he sat up, feeling exceedingly foolish, he looked anxiously at the Cow, expecting to see her laughing at his misfortune, but she stood gazing at him with a very serious expression of countenance, solemnly chewing, and slowly swishing her tail from side to side. As Davy really didn't know how to begin a conversation with a Cow, he waited for her to speak first, and there was consequently a long pause. Presently the Cow said, in a melancholy, lowing tone of voice, "The old gray goose is dead."

"I'm very sorry," said Davy, not knowing what else to say.

"She is," said the Cow, positively, "and we've buried her in the vegetable garden. We thought gooseberries would come up, but they didn't. Nothing came up but feathers."

"That's very curious," said Davy.

"Curious, but comfortable," replied the Cow. "You see, it makes a feather-bed in the garden. The pig sleeps there, and calls it his quill pen. Now *I* think that pig-pens should be made of porcupine quills."

"So do I," said Davy, laughing. "What else is there in the garden?"

"Nothing but the bean-stalk," said the Cow. "You've heard of 'Jack and the Bean-stalk,' haven't you?"

"Oh! yes, indeed!" said Davy, beginning to be very much interested. "I should like to see the bean-stalk."

"You can't *see* the beans talk," said the Cow, gravely. "You might *hear* them talk; that is, if they had anything to say, and you listened long enough. By the way, that's the house that Jack built. Pretty, isn't it?"

Davy turned and looked up at the house. It certainly was a very pretty house, built of bright red brick, with little gables, and dormer-windows in the roof, and with a trim little porch quite overgrown with climbing roses. Suddenly an idea struck him, and he exclaimed: —

"Then you must be the Cow with a crumpled horn!"

"It's not crumpled," said the Cow, with great dignity. "There's a slight crimp in it, to be sure, but nothing that can properly be called a crump. Then the story was all wrong about my tossing the dog. It was the cat that ate the malt. He was a Maltese cat, and his name was Flipmegilder."

"Did you toss *him?*" inquired Davy.

"Certainly not," said the Cow, indignantly. "Who ever heard of a cow tossing a cat? The fact is, I've never had a fair chance to toss *anything.* As for the dog, Mother Hubbard never permitted any liberties to be taken with *him.*"

"I'd dearly love to see Mother Hubbard," said Davy, eagerly.

"Well, you can," said the Cow, indifferently. "She isn't much to see. If you'll look in at the kitchen window you'll probably find her performing on the piano and singing a song. She's always at it."

Davy stole softly to the kitchen window and peeped in, and, as the Cow had said, Mother Hubbard was there, sitting at the piano, and evidently just preparing to sing. The piano was very remarkable, and Davy could not remember ever having seen one like it before. The top of it was arranged with shelves, on which stood all the kitchen crockery, and in the under part of it, at one end, was an oven with glass doors, through which he could see several pies baking.

Mother Hubbard was dressed, just as he expected, in a very ornamental flowered gown, with high-heeled shoes and buckles, and wore a tall pointed hat over her nightcap. She was so like the pictures Davy had seen of her that he thought he would have recognized her anywhere. She sang in a high key with a very quavering voice, and this was the song: —

> *I had an educated pug,*
> * His name was Tommy Jones;*
> *He lived upon the parlor rug*
> * Exclusively on bones.*
>
> *And if, in a secluded room,*
> * I hid one on a shelf,*

It disappeared; so I presume
    He used to help himself.

He had an entertaining trick
    Of feigning he was dead;
Then, with a reassuring kick,
    Would stand upon his head.

I could not take the proper change,
    And go to buy him shoes,
But what he'd sit upon the range
    And read the latest news.

And when I ventured out, one day,
    To order him a coat,
I found him, in his artless way,
    Careering on a goat.

I could not go to look at hats
    But that, with childish glee,
He'd ask in all the neighbors' cats
    To join him at his tea.

And when I went to pay a bill
    (I think it was for tripe),
He made himself extremely ill
    By smoking with a pipe.

There was something about the prim language of this song that sounded very familiar to Davy, and when Mother Hubbard chanced to turn her face towards him he was surprised to see that she looked very like old Miss Peggs, his school-teacher. While she was singing the song little handfuls of gravel were constantly thrown at her through one of the kitchen windows, and by the time the song was finished her lap was quite full of it.

"I'd just like to know who is throwing that gravel," said Davy, indignantly.

"It's Gobobbles," said the Cow, calmly. "You'll find him around at the front of the house. By the way, have you any chewing-gum about you?"

"No," said Davy, greatly surprised at the question.

"So I supposed," said the Cow. "It's precisely what I should expect of a person who would fall out of a window."

"But I couldn't help *that,*" said Davy.

"Of course you couldn't," said the Cow, yawning indolently. 'It's precisely what I should expect of a person who hadn't any chewing-gum.'" And with this the Cow walked gravely away, just as Mother Hubbard made her appearance at the window.

"Boy," said Mother Hubbard, beaming mildly upon Davy through her spectacles, "you shouldn't throw gravel."

"I haven't thrown any," said Davy.

"Fie!" said Mother Hubbard, shaking her head; "always speak the truth."

"I am speaking the truth," said Davy, indignantly. "It was Gobobbles."

"So I supposed," said Mother Hubbard, gently shaking her head again. "It would have been far better if he had been cooked last Christmas instead of being left over. Stuffing him and then letting him go has made a very proud creature of him. You should never be proud."

"I'm not proud," replied Davy, provoked at being mixed up with Gobobbles in this way.

"You may define the word *proud,* and give a few examples," continued Mother Hubbard; and by this time she had grown to be so surprisingly like Miss Peggs that Davy immediately clasped his hands behind him, according to rule, and prepared to recite.

"Proud means being set up, I think," he said, respectfully; "but I don't think I know any examples."

"You may take Gobobbles for an example," replied Mother Hubbard. "You'll find *him* set up in front of the house, and mind you don't aggravate him;" and after again beaming mildly through her spectacles she disappeared from the window, and Davy went cautiously around the corner of the house, curious to see what Gobobbles might be like. As he approached the front of the house he heard a loud, thumping noise, and presently he came in sight of Gobobbles, who proved to be a large and very bold-mannered turkey with all his feathers taken off except a frowsy tuft about his neck. He was tied fast in a baby's high chair, and was thumping his chest with his wings in such a violent and ill-tempered manner that Davy at once made up his mind not to aggravate him under any circumstances. As Gobobbles caught sight of him he discontinued his thumping, and, after staring at him for a moment, said sulkily:—

"I can't abide boys!"

"Why not?" said Davy.

"Oh, they're so hungry!" said Gobobbles, passionately. "They're so everlastingly hungry. Now don't deny that you're fond of turkey."

"Well, I *do* like turkey," said Davy, seeing no way out of the difficulty.

"Of course you do!" said Gobobbles, tossing his head. "Now you might as well know," he continued, resuming his thumping with increased energy, "that I'm as hollow as a

drum and as tough as a hat-box. Just mention that fact to any one you meet, will you? I suppose Christmas is coming, of course."

"Of course it is," replied Davy.

"It's *always* coming!" said Gobobbles, angrily; "I never knew a time yet when it *wasn't* coming!"

"*I* don't mind having it come," said Davy, stoutly.

"Oh, don't you, indeed!" said Gobobbles. "Well, then, *I* don't mind having *you* go!" and here he began hopping his chair forward in such a threatening manner that Davy turned and walked away with as much dignity as he could assume.

As he went around the corner of the house again he found himself in a pleasant lane, bordered on either side by a tall hedge, and, as he was now out of sight of Gobobbles, he started off on a gentle run by way of getting out of the neighborhood as soon as possible. Before he had gone a dozen steps, however, he heard a thumping sound behind him, and, looking back, he saw, to his dismay, that Gobobbles had in some way got loose from his high chair, and was coming after him, thumping himself in a perfect frenzy. In fact, his appearance was so formidable that Davy did not pause for a second look, but started off at the top of his speed.

Gobobbles, however, proved himself to be a capital runner, and, in spite of all Davy's efforts, he could hear the dreadful thumping sound coming nearer and nearer, until it seemed to be just at his heels. At this instant something sprang upon his back; but, before he could cry out in his terror, a head was suddenly thrust over his shoulder, and he found the Goblin, who was now of a bright purple color, staring him in the face and laughing with all his might.

• CHAPTER VI •

THE GIANT BADORFUL

 oblin," said Davy, very seriously, as the little man jumped down from off his back, "if you are going to play such tricks as *that* upon me, I should like to go home at once."

"Where's the harm?" said the Goblin, sitting down on the grass with his back against a wall and smiling contentedly.

"The harm is that I thought it was Gobobbles," said Davy, indignantly.

"Oh, you needn't be afraid of Gobobbles!" said the Goblin. "He's got all that he can attend to, taking care of himself. You see, he's wanted for Christmas, but why anybody should want *him* to eat is more than I can understand. Why, he's seventy years old if he's a day, and as indigestible as an old cork."

Just at this moment a loud, rumbling noise, like distant thunder, came from behind the wall against which the Goblin was leaning, followed by a tremendous sneeze, that fairly shook the ground

"What's that?" whispered Davy to the Goblin, in great alarm.

"It's only Badorful," said the Goblin, laughing. "He's always snoring and waking himself up, and I suppose it's sleeping on the ground that makes him sneeze. Let's have a look at him;" and the Goblin led the way along the wall to a large grating.

Davy looked through the grating, and was much alarmed at seeing a giant, at least twenty feet in height, sitting on the ground, with his legs crossed under him like a tailor. He was dressed in a shabby suit of red velveteen, with a great leathern belt about his waist and enormous boots, and Davy thought he looked terribly ferocious. On the grass beside him lay a huge club, thickly studded at one end with great iron knobs; but Davy noticed, to his great relief, that some little creeping vines were twining themselves among these knobs, and that moss was growing thickly upon one side of the club itself, as though it had been lying there untouched for a long time.

The giant was talking to himself in a low tone, and after listening attentively at the grating for a moment, the Goblin shrieked: "He's making poetry!" and, throwing himself upon the ground, kicked up his heels in a perfect ecstasy of delight.

"Oh, hush, hush!" cried Davy, in terror. "Suppose he hears you!"

"Hears me!" said the Goblin, discontinuing his kicking and looking very much surprised. "What if he does?"

"Well, you know, he *might* not like being laughed at," said Davy, anxiously.

"There's something in that," said the Goblin, staring reflectively at the ground.

"And, you see," continued Davy, "a giant who doesn't like what's going on must be a dreadful creature."

"Oh! there's no fear of *him*," said the Goblin, contemptuously, motioning with his head toward the giant. "He's too old. Why, I must have known him, off and on, for nearly two hundred years. Come in and see him."

"Will he do anything?" said Davy, anxiously.

"Bless you, no!" said the Goblin. "He's a perfect old kitten;" and with these words he pushed open the grating and passed through, with Davy following tremblingly at his heels. Badorful looked up with a feeble smile, and merely said, "Just listen to this:" —

> *My age is three hundred and seventy-two,*
> *And I think, with the deepest regret,*
> *How I used to pick up and voraciously chew*
> *The dear little boys whom I met.*
>
> *I've eaten them raw, in their holiday suits;*
> *I've eaten them curried with rice;*
> *I've eaten them baked, in their jackets and boots,*
> *And found them exceedingly nice.*
>
> *But now that my jaws are too weak for such fare,*
> *I think it exceedingly rude*
> *To do such a thing, when I'm quite well aware*
> *Little boys do not like to be chewed.*
>
> *And so I contentedly live upon eels,*
> *And try to do nothing amiss,*
> *And I pass all the time I can spare from my meals*
> *In innocent slumber—like this.*

Here Badorful rolled over upon his side, and was instantly fast asleep.

"You *see*," said the Goblin, picking up a large stone and thumping with it upon the giant's head, "you *see*, he's quite weak *here;* otherwise, considering his age, he's a very capable giant."

At this moment a farmer, with bright red hair, thrust his head in at the grating, and calling out, "Here comes Gobobbles!" disappeared again; and Davy and the Goblin rushed out, and were just in time to see Gobobbles go by like a flash, with a crowd of people armed with pitch-forks in hot pursuit. Gobobbles was going in fine style, bounding over the hedges and stone-walls like a kangaroo, and thumping vigorously, as usual, with his wings, and Davy and the Goblin were just setting off on a run to join in the chase, when a voice said, "Ahem!" and, looking up, they saw Badorful staring at them over the top of the wall.

"How does *this* strike you?" he said, addressing himself to Davy: —

> *Although I am a giant of the exhibition size,*
> *I've been nicely educated, and I notice with surprise*
> *That the simplest rules of etiquette you don't pretend to keep,*
> *For you skurry off to races while a gentleman's asleep.*
>
> *Don't reply that I was drowsy, for my nap was but a kind*
> *Of dramatic illustration of a peaceful frame of mind;*
> *And you really might have waited till I woke again, instead*
> *Of indelicately pounding, with a stone, upon my head.*
>
> *Very probably you'll argue that our views do not agree, —*
> *I've often found that little boys have disagreed with me, —*
> *But I'm properly entitled, on the compensation plan,*
> *To three times as much politeness as an ordinary man.*

Davy was greatly distressed at having these severe remarks addressed to him. "If you please, sir," he said earnestly, "*I* didn't pound you."
At this the giant glared savagely at the Goblin, and continued: —

> *My remarks have been directed at the one who, I supposed,*
> *Had been violently thumping on my person while I dozed;*
> *By a simple calculation, you will find that there is due*
> *Just six times as much politeness from a little chap like you.*

"Oh! you make me ill!" said the Goblin, flippantly. "Go to sleep."

Badorful stared at him for a moment, and then, with a sickly smile, murmured, "Good-afternoon," and disappeared behind the wall.

Davy and the Goblin now hurried off in pursuit of Gobobbles, and presently came upon the crowd of farmers who had joined hands in a ring, and were dancing around a large white object lying on the ground. Davy pushed his way eagerly through the crowd, expecting to see Gobobbles; but the white object proved to be the Cockalorum hemmed in by a ring of pitchforks sticking in the ground, and with his feathers more rumpled than ever.

"Dear me!" exclaimed Davy, perfectly amazed, "I thought we were chasing Gobobbles!"

"Of course you did," said the Goblin, complacently; "but in this part of the world things very often turn out to be different from what they would have been if they hadn't been otherwise than as you expected they were going to be."

"But you thought so yourself," began Davy, when, to his distress, the Goblin suddenly faded into a dull pinkish color, and then disappeared altogether. Davy looked about him, and found that the Cockalorum and the dancing farmers had also disappeared, and that he was quite alone in a dense wood.

CHAPTER VII

THE MOVING FOREST

h, dear!" cried Davy, speaking aloud in his distress, "I do wish people and things wouldn't change about so! Just so soon as ever I get to a place it goes away, and I'm somewhere else!"—and the little boy's heart began to beat rapidly as he looked about him; for the wood was very dark and solemn and still.

Presently the trees and bushes directly before him moved silently apart and showed a broad path beautifully overgrown with soft turf; and as he stepped forward upon it the trees and bushes beyond moved silently aside in their turn, and the path grew before him, as he walked along, like a green carpet slowly unrolling itself through the wood. It made him a little uneasy, at first, to find that the trees behind him came together again, quietly blotting out the path; but then he thought, "It really doesn't matter, so long as I don't want to go back;" and so he walked along very contentedly.

By and by the path seemed to give itself a shake, and, turning abruptly around a large tree, brought Davy suddenly upon a little butcher's shop, snugly buried in the wood. There was a sign on the shop, reading, "ROBIN HOOD: VENISON," and Robin himself, wearing a clean white apron over his suit of Lincoln green, stood in the door-way, holding a knife and steel, as though he were on the lookout for customers. As he caught sight of Davy he said, "Steaks? Chops?" in an inquiring way, quite like an every-day butcher.

"Venison is deer, isn't it?" said Davy, looking up at the sign.

"Not at all," said Robin Hood, promptly. "it's the cheapest meat about here."

"Oh, I didn't mean that," replied Davy; "I meant that it comes off of a deer."

"Wrong again!" said Robin Hood, triumphantly. "It comes *on* a deer. I cut it off myself. Steaks? Chops?"

"No, I thank you," said Davy, giving up the argument. "I don't think I want anything to eat just now."

"Then what did you come here for?" said Robin Hood, peevishly. "What's the good, I'd like to know, of standing around and staring at an honest tradesman?"

"Well, you see," said Davy, beginning to feel that he had, somehow, been very rude in coming there at all, "I didn't know you were this sort of person at all. I always thought you were an archer, like—like William Tell, you know."

"That's all a mistake about Tell," said Robin Hood, contemptuously. "*He* wasn't an archer. He was a crossbow man,—the crossest one that ever lived. By the way," he added, suddenly returning to business with the greatest earnestness, "you don't happen to want any steaks or chops to-day, do you?"

"No, not to-day, thank you," said Davy, very politely.

"To-morrow?" inquired Robin Hood.

"No, I thank you," said Davy again.

"Will you want any yesterday?" inquired Robin Hood, rather doubtfully.

"I think not," said Davy, beginning to laugh.

Robin Hood stared at him for a moment with a puzzled expression, and then walked into his little shop, and Davy turned away. As he did so the path behind him began to unfold itself through the wood, and, looking back over his shoulder, he saw the little shop swallowed up by the trees and bushes. Just as it disappeared from view he caught a glimpse of a charming little girl, peeping out of a latticed window beside the door. She wore a little red hood, and looked wistfully after Davy as the shop went out of sight.

"I verily believe that was Little Red Riding Hood," said Davy to himself, "and I never knew before that Robin Hood was her father!" The thought of Red Riding Hood, however, brought the wolf to Davy's mind, and he began to anxiously watch the thickets on either side of the path, and even went so far as to whistle softly to himself, by way of showing that he wasn't in the least afraid. He went on and on, hoping the forest would soon come to an end, until the path shook itself again, disclosing to view a trim little brick shop in the densest part of the thicket. It had a neat little green door, with a bright brass knocker upon it, and a sign above it, bearing the words:—

SHAM-SHAM: BARGAINS IN WATCHES.

"Well!" exclaimed Davy, in amazement. "Of all places to sell watches in that's the preposterest!"—but as he turned to walk away he found the trees and bushes for the first time blocking his way, and refusing to move aside. This distressed him very much, until it suddenly occurred to him that this must mean that he was to go into the shop; and, after a moment's hesitation, he went up and knocked timidly at the door with the bright brass knocker. There was no response to the knock, and Davy cautiously pushed open the door and went in.

The place was so dark that at first he could see nothing, although he heard a rattling sound coming from the back part of the shop; but presently he discovered the figure of an old man, busily mixing something in a large iron pot. As Davy approached him he saw that the pot was full of watches, which the old man was stirring with a ladle. The old creature was very curiously dressed, in a suit of rusty green velvet, with little silver buttons sewed over it, and he wore a pair of enormous yellow-leather boots; and Davy was quite alarmed at seeing that a broad leathern belt about his waist was stuck full of old-fashioned knives and pistols. Davy was about to retreat quickly from the shop, when the old man looked up, and said, in a peevish voice:—

"How many watches do you want?"—and Davy saw that he was a very shocking-looking person, with wild, staring eyes, and with a skin as dark as mahogany, as if he had been soaked in something for ever so long.

"How many?" repeated the old man, impatiently.

"If you please," said Davy, "I don't think I'll take any watches to-day. I'll call"—

"Drat 'em!" interrupted the old man, angrily beating the watches with his ladle; "I'll never get rid of em—never!"

"It seems to me"—began Davy, soothingly.

"Of course it does!" again interrupted the old man, as crossly as before. "Of course it does! That's because you won't listen to the why of it."

"But I *will* listen," said Davy.

"Then sit down on the floor and hold up your ears," said the old man.

Davy did as he was told to do, so far as sitting down on the floor was concerned, and the old man pulled a paper out of one of his boots, and, glaring at Davy over the top of it, said, angrily:—

"You're a pretty spectacle! I'm another. What does that make?"

"A pair of spectacles, I suppose," said Davy.

"Right!" said the old man. "Here they are." And pulling an enormous pair of spectacles out of the other boot he put them on, and began reading aloud from his paper:—

> My recollectest thoughts are those
>   Which I remember yet;
> And bearing on, as you'd suppose,
>   The things I don't forget.

> But my resemblest thoughts are less
>   Alike than they should be;
> A state of things, as you'll confess,
>   You very seldom see.

"Clever, isn't it?" said the old man, peeping proudly over the top of the paper.
"Yes, I think it is," said Davy, rather doubtfully.
"Now comes the cream of the whole thing," said the old man. "Just listen to this:"—

> *And yet the mostest thought I love*
> *Is what no one believes—*

Here the old man hastily crammed the paper into his boot again, and stared solemnly at Davy.
"What is it?" said Davy, after waiting a moment for him to complete the verse. The old man glanced suspiciously about the shop, and then added, in a hoarse whisper: —

> *That I'm the sole survivor of*
> *The famous Forty Thieves!*

"But I thought the Forty Thieves were all boiled to death," said Davy.
"All but me," said the old man, decidedly. "I was in the last jar, and when they came to me the oil was off the boil, or the boil was off the oil—I forget which I was—but it ruined my digestion, and made me look like a gingerbread man. What larks we used to have!" he continued, rocking himself back and forth and chuckling hoarsely. "Oh! we were a precious lot, we were! I'm Sham-Sham, you know. Then there was Anamanamona Mike—he was an Irishman from Hullaboo—and Barcelona Boner— he was a Spanish chap, and boned everything he could lay his hands on. Strike's real name was Gobang; but we called him Strike, because he was always asking for more pay. Hare Ware was a poacher, and used to catch Welsh rabbits in a trap; we called him 'Hardware' because he had so much *steal* about him. Good joke, wasn't it?"
"Oh, very!" said Davy, laughing.
"Frown Whack was a scowling fellow with a club," continued Sham-Sham. "My! how he could hit! And Harico and Barico were a couple of bad Society Islanders. Then there was Wee Wo—he was a little Chinese chap, and we used to send him down the chimneys to open front doors for us. He used to say *that* sooted him to perfection. Wac—"
At this moment an extraordinary commotion began among the watches. There was no doubt about it, the pot was boiling, and Sham-Sham, angrily crying out, "Don't tell *me* a watched pot never boils!" sprang to his feet, and, pulling a pair of pistols from his belt, began firing at the watches, which were now bubbling over the side of the pot and rolling about the floor; while Davy, who had had quite enough of Sham-Sham by this time, ran out of the door.
To his great surprise he found himself in a sort of underground passage, lighted

by grated openings overhead; but as he could still hear Sham-Sham, who now seemed to be firing all his pistols at once, he did not hestitate, but ran along the passage at the top of his speed.

Presently he came in sight of a figure hurrying toward him with a lighted candle, and, as it approached, he was perfectly astounded to see that it was Sham-Sham himself, dressed up in a neat calico frock and a dimity apron, like a house-keeper, and with a bunch of keys hanging at his girdle.

The old man seemed to be greatly agitated, and hurriedly whispering, "We thought you were *never* coming, sir!" led the way through the passage in great haste. Davy noticed that they were now in a sort of tunnel made of fine grass. The grass had a delightful fragrance, like new-mown hay, and was neatly wound around the tunnel, like the inside of a bird's-nest. The next moment they came out into an open space in the forest, where, to Davy's amazement the Cockalorum was sitting bolt upright in an arm-chair, with his head wrapped up in flannel.

It seemed to be night, but the place was lighted up by a large chandelier that hung from the branches of a tree, and Davy saw that a number of odd-looking birds were roosting on the chandelier among the lights, gazing down upon the poor Cockalorum with a melancholy interest. As Sham-Sham made his appearance, with Davy at his heels, there was a sudden commotion among the birds, and they all cried out together, "Here's the doctor!" but before Davy could reply, the Hole-keeper suddenly made his appearance, with his great book, and, hurriedly turning over the leaves, said, pointing to Davy, "*He* isn't a doctor. His name is Gloopitch." At these words there arose a long, wailing cry, the lights disappeared, and Davy found himself on a broad path in the forest, with the Hole-keeper walking quietly beside him.

• CHAPTER VIII •

SINDBAD THE SAILOR'S HOUSE

ou had no right to tell those birds my name was Gloopitch!" said Davy, angrily. "That's the second time you've got it wrong."

"Well, it's of no consequence," said the Hole-keeper, complacently. "I'll make it something else the next time. I suppose you know they've caught Gobobbles?"

"I'm glad of it!" said Davy, heartily. "He's worse than the Cockalorum, ten times over. What did they do with him?"

"Cooked him," said the Hole-keeper—"roasted him, fried him, pickled him, and boiled him."

"Gracious!" exclaimed Davy; "I shouldn't think he'd be good for much after all that."

"He isn't," replied the Hole-keeper, calmly. "They're going to keep him to rub out pencil-marks with."

This was such a ridiculous idea that Davy threw back his head, and laughed long and loud.

"Do that again," said the Hole-keeper, stopping short in his walk and gazing at him earnestly; and Davy burst into another fit of laughter.

"Do it again," persisted the Hole-keeper, staring at him still more solemnly.

This was somewhat tiresome; and, after a rather feeble attempt at a third laugh, Davy said, "I don't feel like it any more."

"If *I* could do that," said the Hole-keeper, earnestly, "I'd never stop. The fact is," he continued, gravely shaking his head, "I've never laughed in my life. Does it hurt much?"

"It doesn't hurt at all," said Davy, beginning to laugh again.

"Well, there, there!" said the Hole-keeper, peevishly, resuming his walk again; "don't keep it up *forever*. By the way, you're not the postman, are you?"

"Of course I'm not," said Davy.

"I'm glad of that," said the Hole-keeper; "postmen are always so dreadfully busy. Would you mind delivering a letter for me?" he added, lowering his voice confidentially.

"Oh, no," answered Davy, rather reluctantly; "not if it will be in my way."

"It's sure to be in your way, because it's so big," said the Hole-keeper; and, taking the letter out of his pocket, he handed it to Davy. It certainly was a very large letter, curiously folded, like a dinner-napkin, and sealed in a great many places with red and white peppermint drops, and Davy was much pleased to see that it was addressed: —

> *Captain Robinson Crusoe*
> *Jeran Feranderperandamam,*
> B. G.

"What does B. G. stand for?" said Davy.

"Baldergong's Geography, of course," said the Hole-keeper.

"But why do you put *that* on the letter?" inquired Davy.

"Because you can't find Jeran Feranderperandamam anywhere else, stupid," said the Hole-keeper, impatiently. "But I can't stop to argue about it now;" and, saying this, he turned into a side path, and disappeared in the wood.

As Davy walked mournfully along, turning the big letter over and over in his hands, and feeling very confused by the Hole-keeper's last remark, he presently saw, lying on the walk before him, a small book, beautifully bound in crimson morocco, and, picking it up, he saw that it was marked on the cover: —

> BALDERGONG'S STUFFING FOR THE STUPID

"Perhaps this will tell me where to go," he thought as he opened it; but it proved to be far more confusing than the Hole-keeper himself had been. In fact it was altogether the most ridiculous and provoking book Davy had ever seen.

The first page was headed, in large capital letters: —

HOW TO FRILL GRIDDLEPIGS.

And it seemed to Davy that this *ought* to be something about cooking sausages; but all he found below the heading was: —

Never frill 'em: snuggle 'em always.

And this seemed so perfectly silly that he merely said, "Oh bosh!" and turned impatiently to the next page. This, however, was no better. The heading was:—

TWO WAYS OF FRUMPLING CRUMBLES.

And under this was—

One way:—
Frumple your crumbles with rumbles.
The other way:—
Frumple your crumbles: then add two grumbles of tumbles and stir rapidly.

Davy read this over two or three times, in the greatest perplexity, and then gave it up in despair.

"It's nothing at all except a jumbly way of cooking something tumbly," he said to himself, and then turned sadly to the third page. Alas! this was a great deal worse, being headed:—

THE BEST SNUB FOR FEASTIE SPRALLS;

and poor Davy began to feel as if he were taking leave of his senses. He was just about to throw the book down in disgust, when it was suddenly snatched out of his hands; and, turning hastily, he saw a savage glaring at him from the bushes.

Now Davy knew perfectly well, as all little boys should know, that when you meet a savage in the woods you must get behind a tree as quickly as possible; but he did this in such haste that he found, to his dismay, that he and the savage had chosen the same tree, and in the next instant the savage was after him. The tree was a very large one, and Davy, in his fright, went around it a number of times, so rapidly that he presently caught sight of the back of the savage, and he was surprised to see that he was no bigger than a large monkey; and, moreover, that he was gorgeously dressed, in a beautiful blue coat, with brass buttons on the tail of it, and pink striped trousers. He had hardly made this discovery when the savage vanished as mysteriously as he had appeared, and the next moment Davy came suddenly upon a high paling of logs that began at the tree and extended in a straight line far out into the forest.

It was very puzzling to Davy when it occurred to him that, although he had been around the tree at least a dozen times, he had never seen this paling before, and a door that was in it also bothered him; for, though it was quite an ordinary-looking door, it had no knob nor latch, nor, indeed, any way of being opened that he could perceive. On one side of it, in the paling, was a row of bell-pulls, marked:—

> *Family;*
> *Police;*
> *Butcher;*
> *Baker;*
> *Candlestick-maker;*

and on the door itself was a large knocker, marked: —

Postman.

After examining all these Davy decided that, as he had a letter in charge, he was more of a postman than anything else, and he therefore raised the knocker and rapped loudly. Immediately all the bell-pulls began flying in and out of their own accord, with a deafening clangor of bells behind the paling; and then the door swung slowly back upon its hinges.

Davy walked through the door-way and found himself in the oddest-looking little country place that could possibly be imagined. There was a little lawn laid out, on which a sort of soft fur was growing instead of grass, and here and there about the lawn, in the place of flower-beds, little footstools, neatly covered with carpet, were growing out of the fur. The trees were simply large feather-dusters, with varnished handles; but they seemed, nevertheless, to be growing in a very thriving manner, and on a little mound at the back of the lawn stood a small house, built entirely of big conch-shells, with their pink mouths turned outward. This gave the house a very cheerful appearance, as if it were constantly on a broad grin.

To Davy's dismay, however, the savage was sitting in the shade of one of the dusters, complacently reading the little red book, and he was just wondering whether or not he would be able to get out of the place without being seen, when the little creature looked up at him with a tremendous smile on his face, and Davy saw, to his astonishment, that he was the Goblin, dressed up like an Ethiopian serenader.

"Oh! you dear, delicious old Goblin!" cried Davy, in an ecstasy of joy at again finding his travelling-companion. "And were you the savage that was chasing me just now?"

The Goblin nodded his head, and, exclaiming "My, how you did cut and run!" rolled over and over, kicking his heels about in a delirium of enjoyment.

"Goblin," said Davy, gravely, "I think we could have just as good a time without any such doings as that."

"*I* couldn't," said the Goblin, sitting up again and speaking very positively; "It's about all the fun I have."

"Well, then," said Davy, "I wish you wouldn't be disappearing all the time. I think that is a very disagreeable habit."

"Rubbish!" said the Goblin, with a chuckle. "That's only my way of getting a vacation."

"And where do you go?" inquired Davy; but this proved to be a very unfortunate question, for the Goblin immediately began fading away in such an alarming manner that he would certainly have gone entirely out of sight if Davy had not caught him by the coat-collar and pulled him into view again with a gentle shake.

"Oh, I beg your pardon!" said Davy, who was greatly alarmed by this narrow escape. "I really don't care to know about that; I only want to know what place this is."

The Goblin stared about him in a dazed manner for a moment, and then said, "Sindbad the Sailor's house."

"Really and truly?" said the delighted Davy.

"Really and treally truly," said the Goblin. "And here he comes now!"

Davy looked around and saw an old man coming toward them across the lawn. He was dressed in a Turkish costume, and wore a large turban and red morocco slippers turned up at the toes like skates; and his white beard was so long that at every fourth step he trod upon it and fell flat on his face. He took no notice whatever of either Davy or the Goblin, and, after falling down a number of times, took his seat upon one of the little carpet footstools, and taking off his turban began stirring about in it with a large wooden spoon. As he took off his turban Davy saw that his head, which was prefectly bald, was neatly laid out in black and white squares like a chess-board.

"This here Turk is the most reckless old story-teller that ever was born," said the Goblin, pointing with his thumb over his shoulder at Sindbad. "You can't believe half he tells you."

"I'd like to hear one of his stories, for all that," said Davy.

"All right!" said the Goblin, promptly; "just come along with me, and he'll give us a whopper."

As they started off to join Sindbad, Davy was much surprised to see that the Goblin was much taller than he had been; in fact, he was now almost up to Davy's shoulder.

"Why, I verily believe you've been growing!" exclaimed Davy, staring at him in amazement.

"I have," said the Goblin, calmly. "But I only did it to fit these clothes. It's much handier, you see, than having a suit made to order."

"But, suppose the clothes had been too small?" argued Davy.

"Then I'd have grown the other way," replied the Goblin, with an immense smile. "It doesn't make a bit of difference to me which way I grow. Anything to be comfortable is my rule;" and as he said this they came to where Sindbad was sitting, busily stirring with his great spoon.

As Davy and the Goblin sat down beside him, Sindbad hastily put on his turban,

and, after scowling at Davy for a moment, said to the Goblin, "It's no use telling *him* anything; he's as deaf as a trunk."

"Then tell it to me," said the Goblin, with great presence of mind.

"All right," said Sindbad, "I'll give you a nautical one."

Here he rose for a moment, hitched up his big trousers like a sailor, cocked his turban on one side of his head, and, sitting down again, began: —

A capital ship for an ocean trip
      Was "The Walloping Window-blind;"
No gale that blew dismayed her crew
      Or troubled the captain's mind.
The man at the wheel was taught to feel
      Contempt for the wildest blow,
And it often appeared, when the weather had cleared,
      That he'd been in his bunk below.

The boatswain's mate was very sedate,
      Yet fond of amusement, too;
And he played hop-scotch with the starboard watch
      While the captain tickled the crew.
And the gunner we had was apparently mad,
      For he sat on the after-rail,
And fired salutes with the captain's boots,
      In the teeth of the booming gale.

The captain sat in a commodore's hat,
      And dined, in a royal way
On toasted pigs and pickles and figs
      And gummery bread, each day.
But the cook was Dutch, and behaved as such;
      For the food that he gave the crew
Was a number of tons of hot-cross buns,
      Chopped up with sugar and glue.

And we all felt ill as mariners will,
      On a diet that's cheap and rude;
And we shivered and shook as we dipped the cook
      In a tub of his gluesome food.
Then nautical pride we laid aside,

And we cast the vessel ashore
On the Gulliby Isles, where the Poohpooh smiles,
    And the Anagazanders roar.

Composed of sand was that favored land,
    And trimmed with cinnamon straws;
And pink and blue was the pleasing hue
    Of the Tickletoeteaser's claws.
And we sat on the edge of a sandy ledge
    And shot at the whistling bee;
And the Binnacle-bats wore water-proof hats
    As they danced in the sounding sea.

On rubagub bark, from dawn to dark,
    We fed, till we all had grown
Uncommonly shrunk—when a Chinese junk
    Came by from the torriby zone.
She was stubby and square, but we didn't much care,
    And we cheerily put to sea;
And we left the crew of the junk to chew
    The bark of the rubagub tree.

Here Sindbad stopped, and gazed solemnly at Davy and the Goblin.

"If you please, sir," said Davy, respectfully, "what is gummery bread?"

"It's bread stuffed with molasses," said Sindbad; "but I never saw it anywhere except aboard of 'The Prodigal Pig.'"

"But," said Davy, in great surprise, "you said the name of your ship was"—

"So I did, and so it was," interrupted Sindbad, testily. "The name of a ship sticks to it like wax to a wig. You *can't* change it."

"Who gave it that name?" said the Goblin.

"What name?" said Sindbad, looking very much astonished.

"Why, 'The Cantering Soup-tureen,'" said the Goblin, winking at Davy.

"Oh, *that* name," said Sindbad,—"that was given to her by the Alamagoozelum of Popjaw. But speaking of soup-tureens, let's go and have some pie;" and, rising to his feet, he gave one hand to Davy and the other to the Goblin, and they all walked off in a row toward the little shell house. This, however, proved to be a very troublesome arrangement, for Sindbad was constantly stepping on his long beard and falling down; and as he kept a firm hold of his companions' hands they all went down in a heap together a great many times. At last Sindbad's turban fell off, and as he sat up on the grass, and began stirring in it again with his wooden spoon, Davy saw that it was full of broken chessmen.

"It's a great improvement, isn't it?" said Sindbad.

"What is?" said Davy, very much puzzled.

"Why, this way of playing the game," said Sindbad, looking up at him complacently. "You see, you make all the moves at once."

"It must be a very easy way," said Davy.

"It's nothing of the sort," said Sindbad, sharply. "There are more moves in one of my games than in twenty ordinary games;" and here he stirred up the chessmen furiously for a moment, and then triumphantly calling out "Check!" clapped the turban on his head.

As they set out again for the little house, Davy saw that it was slowly moving around the edge of the lawn, as if it were on a circular railway, and Sindbad followed it around, dragging Davy and the Goblin with him, but never getting any nearer to the house.

"Don't you think," said Davy, after awhile, "that it would be a good plan to stand still and wait until the house came around to us?"

"Here, drop that!" exclaimed Sindbad, excitedly; "that's my idea. I was just about proposing it myself."

"So was I," said the Goblin to Sindbad. "Just leave my ideas alone, will you?"

"*Your* ideas!" retorted Sindbad, scornfully. "I didn't know you'd brought any with you."

"I had to," replied the Goblin, with great contempt, "otherwise there wouldn't have been any on the premises."

"Oh! come, I say!" cried Sindbad; "that's my sneer, you know. Don't go to putting the point of it the wrong way."

"Take it back, if it's the only one you have," retorted the Goblin, with another wink at Davy.

"Thank you , I believe I will," replied Sindbad, meekly; and, as the little house came along just then, they all stepped in at the door as it went by. As they did so, to Davy's amazement, Sindbad and the Goblin quietly vanished, and Davy, instead of being inside the house, found himself standing in a dusty road, quite alone.

• CHAPTER IX •

LAY-OVERS FOR MEDDLERS

s Davy stood in the road, in doubt which way to go, a Roc came around the corner of the house. She was a large bird, nearly six feet tall, and was comfortably dressed, in a bonnet and a plaid shawl, and wore overshoes. About her neck was hung a covered basket and a door-key; and Davy at once concluded that she was Sindbad's house-keeper.

"I didn't mean to keep you waiting," said the Roc, leading the way along the road; "but I declare that, what with combing that lawn every morning with a fine-tooth comb, and brushing those shells every evening with a fine tooth-brush, I don't get time for anything else, let alone feeding the animals."

"What animals?" said Davy, beginning to be interested.

"Why, *his,* of course," said the Roc, rattling on in her harsh voice. "There's an Emphasis and two Periodicals, and a Spotted Disaster, all crawlin' and creepin' and screechin'"—

Here Davy, unable to control himself, burst into a fit of laughter, in which the Roc joined heartily, rolling her head from side to side, and repeating, "All crawlin' and creepin' and screechin,'" over and over again, as if that were the cream of the joke. Suddenly she stopped laughing, and said in a low voice, "You don't happen to have a beefsteak about you, do you?"

Davy confessed that he had not, and the Roc continued, "Then I must go back. Just hold my basket, like a good child." Here there was a scuffling sound in the basket, and the Roc rapped on the cover with her hard beak, and cried, "Hush!"

"What's in it?" said Davy, cautiously taking the basket.

"Lay-overs for meddlers," said the Roc, and, hurrying back along the road, was soon out of sight.

"I wonder what they're like," said Davy to himself, getting down upon his hands and knees and listening curiously with his ear against the cover of the basket. The scuf-fling sound continued, mingled with little sneezes and squeaking sobs, as if some very small kittens had bad colds and were crying about it.

"I think I'll take a peep," said Davy, looking cautiously about him. There was no one in sight, and he carefully raised the cover a little way and tried to look in. The scuffling sound and the sobs ceased, and the next instant the cover flew off the basket, and out poured a swarm of little brown creatures, like snuff-boxes with legs. As they scampered off in all directions Davy made a frantic grab at one of them, when it instantly turned over on its back and blew a puff of smoke into his face, and he rolled over in the road, almost stifled. When he was able to sit up again and look about him, the empty basket was lying on its side near him, and not a lay-over was to be seen. At that moment the Roc came in sight, hurrying along the road with her shawl and her bonnet-strings fluttering behind her; and Davy, clapping the cover on the basket, took to his heels and ran for dear life.

• CHAPTER X •

RIBSY

he road was very dreary and dusty, and wound in and out in the most tiresome way until it seemed to have no end to it, and Davy ran on and on, half expecting at any moment to feel the Roc's great beak pecking at his back. Fortunately his legs carried him along so remarkably well that he felt he could run for a week; and, indeed, he might have done so if he had not, at a sharp turn in the road, come suddenly upon a horse and cab. The horse was fast asleep when Davy dashed against him, but he woke up with a start, and, after whistling like a locomotive once or twice in a very alarming manner, went to sleep again. He was a very frowsy-looking horse, with great lumps at his knees and a long, crooked neck like a camel's; but what attracted Davy's attention particularly was the word "RIBSY" painted in whitewash on his side in large letters. He was looking at this, and wondering if it were the horse's name, when the door of the cab flew open and a man fell out, and, after rolling over in the dust, sat up in the middle of the road and began yawning. He was even a more ridiculous-looking object than the horse, being dressed in a clown's suit, with a morning-gown over it by way of a topcoat, and a field-marshal's cocked hat. In fact, if he had not had a whip in his hand no one would ever have taken him for a cabman. After yawning heartily he looked up at Davy, and said drowsily, "Where to?"

"To B. G.," said Davy, hastily referring to the Hole-keeper's letter.

"All right," said the cabman, yawning again. "Climb in, and don't put your feet on the cushions."

Now, this was a ridiculous thing for him to say, for when Davy stepped inside he found the only seats were some three-legged stools huddled together in the back part of the cab, all the rest of the space being taken up by a large bath-tub that ran across the front end of it. Davy turned on one of the faucets, but nothing came out except some dust and a few small bits of gravel, and he shut it off again, and, sitting down on one of the little stools, waited patiently for the cab to start.

Just then the cabman put his head in at the window, and, winking at him confidentially, said, "Can you tell me why this horse is like an umbrella?"

"No," said Davy.

"Because he's used *up*," said the cabman.

"I don't think that's a very good conundrum," said Davy.

"So do I," said the cabman. "But it's the best one I can make with this horse. Did you say N. B.?" he asked.

"No, I said B. G.," said Davy.

"All right," said the cabman again, and disappeared from the window. Presently there was a loud trampling overhead, and Davy, putting his head out at the window, saw that the cabman had climbed up on top of the cab and was throwing stones at the horse, which was still sleeping peacefully.

"It's all right," said the cabman, cheerfully, as he caught sight of Davy. "If he doesn't start pretty soon I'll give him some snuff. That *always* wakes him up."

"Oh! don't do that," said Davy, anxiously. "I'd rather get out and walk."

"Well, I wish you would," said the cabman, in a tone of great relief. "This is a very valuable stand, and I don't care to lose my place on it;" and Davy accordingly jumped out of the cab and walked away.

Presently there was a clattering of hoofs behind him, and Ribsy came galloping along the road, with nothing on him but his collar. He was holding his big head high in the air, like a giraffe, and gazing proudly about him as he ran. He stopped short when he saw the little boy, and, giving a triumphant whistle, said cheerfully, "How are you again?"

It seemed rather strange to be spoken to by a cab-horse, but Davy answered that he was feeling quite well.

"So am I," said Ribsy. "The fact is, that when it comes to beating a horse about the head with a three-legged stool, if that horse is going to leave at all, it's time he was off."

"I should think it was," said Davy, earnestly.

"You'll observe, of course, that I've kept on my shoes and my collar," said Ribsy. "It isn't genteel to go barefoot, and nothing makes a fellow look so untidy as going about without a collar. The truth is," he continued, sitting down in the road on his hind legs, — "the truth is, I'm not an ordinary horse, by any means. I have a history, and I've arranged it in a popular form, in six canters, —I mean cantos," he added, hastily correcting himself.

"I'd like to hear it, if you please," said Davy, politely.

"Well, I'm a little hoarse," —began Ribsy.

"I think you're a very big horse," said Davy, in great surprise.

"I'm referring to my voice," said Ribsy, haughtily. "Be good enough not to interrupt me again;" and, giving two or three preliminary whistles to clear his throat, he began: —

It's very confining, this living in stables,
And passing one's time among wagons and carts;
I much prefer dining at gentlemen's tables,
And living on turkeys and cranberry tarts.

I find with surprise that I'm constantly sneezing;
I'm stiff in the legs, and I'm often for sale;
And the blue-bottle flies, with their tiresome teasing,
Are quite out of reach of my weary old tail.

"By the way," said Ribsy, getting up and turning himself around, "what does my tail look like?"

"I think," said Davy, after a careful inspection, "I think it looks something like an old paint-brush."

"So I supposed," said Ribsy, gloomily, and, sitting down again, he went on with his history: —

As spry as a kid and as trim as a spider
Was I in the days of the Turnip-top Hunt,
When I used to get rid of the weight of my rider
And canter contentedly in at the front.

I never was told that this jocular feature
Of mine was a trick reprehensibly rude,
And yet I was sold, like a commonplace creature,
To work in a circus for lodgings and food.

"I suppose you have never been a circus-horse?" said Ribsy, stopping short in his verses again and gazing inquiringly at Davy.

"Never," said Davy.

"Then you don't know anything about it," said Ribsy. "Here we go again:" —

Pray why, if you please, should a capable charger
Perform on a ladder and prance in a show?
And why should his knees be made thicker and larger
By teaching him tricks that he'd rather not know?

Oh! why should a horse, for society fitted,
    Be doomed to employment so utterly bad,
And why should a coarse-looking man be permitted
    To dance on his back on a top-heavy pad?

Here Ribsy paused once more, and Davy, feeling that he ought to make some sort of an answer to such a lot of questions, said helplessly, "I don't know."

"No more do I," said Ribsy, tossing his head scornfully.

It made me a wreck, with no hope of improvement,
    Too feeble to race with an invalid crab;
I'm wry in the neck, with a rickety movement
    Peculiarly suited for drawing a cab.

They pinch me with straps, and they bruise me with buckles,
    They drive me too rapidly over the stones; —
A reason, perhaps, why a number of knuckles
    Have lately appeared on my prominent bones.

"I see them," cried Davy, eagerly; "I thought they were corns."

"Thank you," said Ribsy, haughtily. "As the next verse is the last you needn't trouble yourself to make any further observations."

I dream of a spot which I used to roam over
    In infancy's days, with a frolicsome skip,
Content with my lot, which was planted with clover,
    And never annoyed by the crack of a whip.

But I think my remarks will determine the question,
    Of why I am bony and thin as a rail;
I'm off for some larks, to improve my digestion,
    And point the stern moral conveyed by my tail.

Here Ribsy got upon his legs again, and, after a refreshing fillip with his heels, cantered off along the road, whistling as he went. Two large blue-bottle flies were on his back, and his tail was flying around, with an angry whisk, like a pin-wheel; but, as he disappeared in the distance, the flies were still sitting calmly on the ridge of his spine, apparently enjoying the scenery.

Davy was about to start out again on his journey, when he heard a voice shouting

"Hi! Hi!" and, looking back, he saw the poor cabman coming along the road on a brisk trot, dragging his cab after him. He had on Ribsy's harness, and seemed to be in a state of tremendous excitement.

As he came up with Davy the door of the cab flew open again, and the three-legged stools came tumbling out, followed by a dense cloud of dust.

"Get in! Get in!" shouted the cabman, excitedly. "Never mind the dust; I've turned it on to make believe we're going tremendously fast."

Davy hastily scrambled in, and the cabman started off again. The dust was pouring out of both faucets, and a heavy shower of gravel was rattling into the bath-tub; and, to make matters worse, the cabman was now going along at such an astonishing speed that the cab rocked violently from side to side, like a boat in a stormy sea. Davy made a frantic attempt to shut off the dust, but it seemed to come faster and faster, until he was almost choked, and by this time the gravel had become as large as cherry-stones, and was flying around in the cab and rattling about his ears like a little hail-storm. Now, all this was a great deal more than Davy had bargained for, and it was so very unpleasant that he presently sat down on the floor of the cab in hope of getting a little out of the way of the flying gravel. As he did this the rocking motion became less violent, and then ceased altogether, as though the cabman had suddenly come to a stop. Then the dust cleared away, and Davy, to his surprise, found himself sitting in the road directly in front of the little house that Jack built.

The cabman and his cab had vanished entirely, but, curiously enough, the cab door was standing wide open in the wall of the house, just above the porch, and in the opening stood the red Cow gazing down upon him, and solemnly chewing, as before. The house had such a familiar look to him that Davy felt quite at home; and, moreover, the Cow seemed quite like an old acquaintance, compared with the other creatures he had met, and he was just about to begin a friendly conversation with her, when she suddenly stopped chewing, and said, "How did *you* get here?"

"I came in a cab," said Davy. "We came along just behind the horse."

"People in cabs usually do," said the Cow; "leastwise I never heard of any of 'em being ahead of him."

"But this horse was running away, you know," said Davy.

"Where was the cabman?" said the Cow, suspiciously.

"He was drawing the cab," said Davy.

"What!" exclaimed the Cow, —"while the horse was running away? Oh, come, I say!"

"He was, truly," said Davy, laughing; "you never saw anything half so ridiculous."

"I certainly never did—that I can remember," said the Cow; "but then, you see, I haven't always been a cow."

"Really?" said Davy.

"Really," said the Cow, very solemnly. "The fact is, I've been changed."

"And what did you use to be?" said Davy, who was now fully prepared for something marvellous.

"A calf," said the Cow, with a curious rumbling chuckle.

"I don't think *that's* a very good joke," said the disappointed little boy.

"It's a deal funnier than your cab story," said the Cow. "And, what's more, it's true! Good-afternoon." And with this the Cow disappeared from the opening, and the cab door shut to with a loud bang.

Davy sat still for a moment, hoping that Mother Hubbard, or perhaps the dog, or even the cat, would appear, so that he might explain his story about the cab. None of them came; but meanwhile a very extraordinary thing happened, for the house itself began to *go*. First the chimneys sank down through the roof, as if they were being lowered into the cellar. Then the roof itself, with its gables and dormer windows, softly folded itself flat down upon the top of the house, out of sight. Then the cab door and the latticed windows fluttered gently for a moment, as if rather uncertain how to dispose of themselves, and finally faded away, one by one, as if they had been soaked into the bricks. Then the porch gravely took itself to pieces and carried itself, so to speak, carefully in through the front door; and finally the door went in itself, and nothing was left of the house that Jack built but a high brick wall, with the climbing roses running all over it like a beautiful pink vine. All this was so unexpected and so wonderful that Davy sat quite still, expecting something marvellous of this wall; but it proved to be a very matter-of-fact affair, with no intention whatever of doing anything or going anywhere, and, after watching it attentively for a few moments, Davy got up and resumed his journey along the road.

• CHAPTER XI •

ROBINSON CRUSOE'S ISLAND

his is a very sloppy road," said Davy to himself, as he walked away from the Bean-stalk farm; and it was, indeed, a *very* sloppy road. The dust had quite disappeared, and the sloppiness soon changed to such a degree of wetness that Davy presently found himself in water up to his ankles. He turned to go back, and saw, to his alarm, that the land in *every* direction seemed to be miles away, and the depth of the water increased so rapidly that, before he could make up his mind what to do, it had risen to his shoulders, and he was carried off his feet and found himself apparently drifting out to sea. The water, however, was warm and pleasant, and he discovered that, instead of sinking, he was floated gently along, slowly turning in the water like a float on a fishing-line. This was very agreeable; but he was, nevertheless, greatly relieved when a boat came in sight sailing toward him. As it came near, it proved to be the clock, with a sail hoisted, and the Goblin sitting complacently in the stern.

"How d'ye do, Gobsy?" said Davy.

"Prime!" said the Goblin, enthusiastically.

"Well, stop the clock," said Davy; "I want to get aboard."

"I haven't any board," said the Goblin, in great surprise.

"I mean I want to get into the clock," said Davy, laughing. "I don't think you're much of a sailor."

"I'm not," said the Goblin, as Davy climbed in. "I've been sailing one way for ever so long, because I don't know how to turn around; but there's a landing-place just ahead."

Davy looked over his shoulder and found that they were rapidly approaching a little wooden pier, standing about a foot out of the water. Beyond it stretched a broad expanse of sandy beach.

"What place is it?" said Davy.

"It's called Hickory Dickory Dock," said the Goblin. "All the eight-day clocks stop here;" and at this moment the clock struck against the timbers with a violent thump, and Davy was thrown out, heels over head, upon the dock. He scrambled upon his feet again as quickly as possible, and saw, to his dismay, that the clock had been turned completely around by the shock and was rapidly rifting out to sea again. The Goblin looked back despairingly, and Davy just caught the words, "I don't know how to turn around!" when the clock was carried out of hearing distance, and soon disappeared on the horizon.

The beach was covered in every direction with little hills of sand, like haycocks, with scraggy bunches of sea-weed sticking out of the tops of them; and Davy was wondering how they came to be there, when he caught sight of a man walking along the edge of the water, and now and then stopping and gazing earnestly out to sea. As the man drew nearer, Davy saw that he was dressed in a suit of brown leather, and wore a high-peaked hat, and that a little procession, consisting of a dog, a cat, and a goat, was following patiently at his heels, while a parrot was perched upon his shoulder. They all wore very large linen collars and black cravats, which gave them a very serious appearance.

Davy was morally certain that the man was Robinson Crusoe. He carried an enormous gun, which he loaded from time to time, and then, aiming carefully at the sea, fired. There was nothing very alarming about this, for the gun, when fired, only gave a faint squeak, and the bullet, which was about the size of a small orange, dropped out quietly upon the sand. Robinson, for it was really he, always seemed to be greatly astonished at this result, peering long and anxiously down into the barrel of the gun, and sometimes listening attentively, with his ear at the muzzle. His animal companions, however, seemed to be greatly alarmed whenever he prepared to fire; and, scampering off, hid behind the little hills of sand until the gun was discharged, when they would return, and, after solemnly watching their master reload his piece, follow him along the beach as before. This was all so ridiculous that Davy had great difficulty in keeping a serious expression on his face as he walked up to Robinson and handed him the Hole-keeper's letter. Robinson looked at him suspiciously as he took it, and the animals eyed him with evident distrust.

Robinson had some difficulty in opening the letter, which was sopping wet, and took a long time to read it, Davy, meanwhile, waiting patiently. Sometimes Robinson would scowl horribly, as if puzzled, and then, again, he would chuckle to himself, as if vastly amused with the contents; but as he turned the letter over, in reading it, Davy could not help seeing that it was simply a blank sheet of paper, with no writing whatever upon it except the address. This, however, was so like the Hole-keeper's way of doing things that Davy was not much surprised when Robinson remarked. "He has left out the greatest lot of comical things!" and, stooping down, buried the letter in the sand.

Then, picking up his gun, he said, "You may walk about in the grove as long as you please, provided you don't pick anything."

"What grove?" said Davy, very much surprised.

"This one," said Robinson, proudly pointing out the tufts of sea-weed. "They're beach-trees, you know; I planted 'em myself. I had to have some place to go shooting in, of course."

"Can you shoot with *that* gun?" said Davy.

"Shoot! Why, it's a splendid gun!" said Robinson, gazing at it proudly. "I made it myself—out of a spy-glass."

"It doesn't seem to go off," said Davy, doubtfully.

"That's the beauty of it!" exclaimed Robinson, with great enthusiasm. "Some guns go off, and you never see 'em again."

"But I mean that it doesn't make any noise," persisted Davy.

"Of course it doesn't," said Robinson. "That's because I load it with tooth-powder."

"But I don't see what you can shoot with it," said Davy, feeling that he was somehow getting the worst of the argument.

Robinson stood gazing thoughtfully at him for a moment, while the big bullet rolled out of the gun with a rumbling sound and fell into the sea. "I see what you want," he said, at length. "You're after my personal history. Just take a seat in the family circle and I'll give it to you."

Davy looked around and saw that the dog, the goat, and the cat were seated respectfully in a semicircle, with the parrot, which had dismounted, sitting beside the dog. He seated himself on the sand at the other end of the line, and Robinson began as follows:—

> *The night was thick and hazy*
> *When the "Piccadilly Daisy"*
> *Carried down the crew and captain in the sea;*
> *And I think the water drowned 'em;*
> *For they never, never found 'em,*
> *And I know they didn't come ashore with me.*

> *Oh! 'twas very sad and lonely*
> *When I found myself the only*
> *Population on this cultivated shore;*
> *But I've made a little tavern*
> *In a rocky little cavern,*
> *And I sit and watch for people at the door.*

I spent no time in looking
For a girl to do my cooking,
As I'm quite a clever hand at making stews;
But I had that fellow Friday,
Just to keep the tavern tidy,
And to put a Sunday polish on my shoes.

I have a little garden
That I'm cultivating lard in,
As the things I eat are rather tough and dry;
For I live on toasted lizards,
Prickly pears, and parrot gizzards,
And I'm really very fond of beetle-pie.

The clothes I had were furry,
And it made me fret and worry
When I found the moths were eating off the hair;
And I had to scrape and sand 'em,
And I boiled 'em and I tanned 'em,
Till I got the fine morocco suit I wear.

I sometimes seek diversion
In a family excursion
With the few domestic animals you see;
And we take along a carrot
As refreshment for the parrot,
And a little can of jungleberry tea.

Then we gather, as we travel,
Bits of moss and dirty gravel,
And we chip off little specimens of stone;
And we carry home as prizes
Funny bugs, of handy sizes,
Just to give the day a scientific tone.

If the roads are wet and muddy
We remain at home and study, —
For the Goat is very clever at a sum, —

And the Dog, instead of fighting,
Studies ornamental writing,
While the Cat is taking lessons on the drum.

We retire at eleven,
And we rise again at seven;
And I wish to call attention, as I close,
To the fact that all the scholars
Are correct about their collars,
And particular in turning out their toes.

Here Robinson called out, in a loud voice, "First class in arithmetic!" but the animals sat perfectly motionless, sedately staring at him.

"Oh! by the way," said Robinson, confidentially to Davy, "this *is* the first class in arithmetic. That's the reason they didn't move, you see. Now, then," he continued sharply, addressing the class, "how many halves are there in a whole?"

There was a dead silence for a moment, and then the Cat said gravely, "What kind of a hole?"

"That has nothing to do with it," said Robinson, impatiently.

"Oh! hasn't it, though!" exclaimed the Dog, scornfully. "I should think a big hole could have more halves in it than a little one."

"Well, *rather,*" put in the Parrot, contemptuously.

Here the Goat, who apparently had been carefully thinking the matter over, said in a low, quavering voice, "Must all the halves be of the same size?"

"Certainly not," said Robinson, promptly; then, nudging Davy with his elbow, he whispered, "He's bringing his mind to bear on it. He's prodigious when he gets started!"

"Who taught him arithmetic?" said Davy, who was beginning to think Robinson didn't know much about it himself.

"Well, the fact is," said Robinson, confidentially, "he picked it up from an old Adder, that he met in the woods."

Here the Goat, who evidently was not yet quite started, inquired, "Must all the halves be of the same shape?"

"Not at all," said Robinson, cheerfully. "Have 'em any shape you like."

"Then I give it up," said the Goat.

"So do I," said the Dog.

"And I," said the Cat.

"Me, too," said the Parrot.

"Well!" exclaimed Davy, quite out of patience. "You are certainly the stupidest lot of creatures I ever saw."

At this the animals stared mournfully at him for a moment, and then rose up and walked gravely away.

"Now you've spoiled the exercises," said Robinson, peevishly. "I'm sorry I gave 'em such a staggerer to begin with."

"Pooh!" said Davy, contemptuously. "If they couldn't do that sum they couldn't do anything."

Robinson gazed at him admiringly for a moment, and then, looking cautiously about him, to make sure that the procession was out of hearing, said coaxingly:—

"What's the right answer? Tell us, like a good fellow."

"Two, of course," said Davy.

"Is that all?" exclaimed Robinson, in a tone of great astonishment.

"Certainly," said Davy, who began to feel very proud of his learning. "Don't you know that when they divide a whole into four parts they call them fourths, and when they divide it into two parts they call them halves?"

"Why don't they call them tooths?" said Robinson, obstinately. "The fact is, they ought to call 'em teeth. That's what puzzled the Goat. Next time I'll say, 'How many teeth in a whole?'"

"Then the Cat will ask if it's a rat-hole," said Davy, laughing at the idea.

"You positively convulse me, you're so very humorous," said Robinson, without a vestige of a smile. "You're almost as droll as Friday was. He used to call the Goat 'Pat,' because he said he was a little butter. I told him that was altogether too funny for a lonely place like this, and he went away and joined the minstrels."

Here Robinson suddenly turned pale, and, hastily reaching out for his gun, sprang to his feet.

Davy looked out to sea, and saw that the clock, with the Goblin standing in the stern, had come in sight again, and was heading directly for the shore with tremendous speed. The poor Goblin, who had turned sea-green in color, was frantically waving his hands to and fro, as if motioning for the beach to get out of the way; and Davy watched his approach with the greatest anxiety. Meanwhile the animals had mounted on four sand-hills, and were solemnly looking on, while Robinson, who seemed to have run out of tooth-powder, was hurriedly loading his gun with sand. The next moment the clock struck the beach with great force, and, turning completely over on the sand, buried the Goblin beneath it. Robinson was just making a convulsive effort to fire off his gun, when the clock began striking loudly, and he and the animals fled in all directions in the wildest dismay.

• CHAPTER XII •

A WHALE IN A WAISTCOAT

avy rushed up to the clock, and, pulling open the little door in the front of it, looked inside. To his great disappointment the Goblin had again disappeared, and there was a smooth, round hole running down into the sand, as though he had gone directly through the beach. He was listening at this hole, in the hope of hearing from the Goblin, when a voice said, "I suppose that's what they call going into the interior of the country;" and, looking up, he saw the Hole-keeper sitting on a little mound in the sand, with his great book in his lap.

The little man had evidently been having a hard time since Davy had seen him. His complexion had quite lost its beautiful transparency, and his jaunty little paper tunic was sadly rumpled, and moreover, he had lost his cocked hat. All this, however, had not at all disturbed his complacent conceit; he was, if anything, more pompous than ever.

"How did *you* get here?" asked Davy, in astonishment.

"I'm banished," said the Hole-keeper, cheerfully. "That's better than being boiled, any day. Did you give Robinson my letter?"

"Yes, I did," said Davy, as they walked along the beach together; "but I got it very wet coming here."

"That was quite right," said the Hole-keeper. "There's nothing so tiresome as a dry letter. Well, I suppose Robinson is expecting me by this time, isn't he?"

"I don't know, I'm sure," said Davy. "He didn't say that he was expecting you."

"He *must* be," said the Hole-keeper, positively. "I never even mentioned it in my letter; so, of course, he'll know I'm coming. By the way," he added, hurriedly opening his book, and staring anxiously at one of the blank pages, "there isn't a word in here about Billyweazles. This place must be full of 'em."

"What are they?" said Davy.

"They're great pink birds, without any feathers on 'em," replied the Hole-keeper, solemnly. "And they're particularly fond of sugar. That's the worst thing about 'em."

"I don't think there's anything very wicked in that," said Davy.

"Oh! of course *you* don't," said the Hole-keeper, fretfully. "But you see I haven't any trowsers on, and I don't fancy have a lot of strange Billyweazles nibbling at my legs. In fact, if you don't mind, I'd like to run away from here."

"Very well," said Davy, who was himself beginning to feel rather nervous about the Billyweazles, and accordingly he and the Hole-keeper started off along the beach as fast as they could run.

Presently the Hole-keeper stopped short and said, faintly, "It strikes me the sun is very hot here."

The sun certainly was very hot, and Davy, looking at the Hole-keeper as he said this, saw that his face was gradually and very curiously losing its expression, and that his nose had almost entirely disappeared.

"What's the matter?" inquired Davy anxiously.

"The matter is that I'm going back into the raw material," said the Hole-keeper, dropping his book, and sitting down helplessly in the sand. "See here, Frinkles," he continued, beginning to speak very thickly; "wrap me up in my shirt and mark the packish distingly. Take off shir quigly!" and Davy had just time to pull the poor creature's shirt over his head and spread it quickly on the beach, when the Hole-keeper fell down, rolled over upon the garment, and, bubbling once or twice, as if he were boiling, melted away into a compact lump of brown sugar.

Davy was deeply affected by this sad incident, and, though he had never really liked the Hole-keeper, he could hardly keep back his tears as he wrapped up the lump in the paper shirt and laid it carefully on the big book. In fact, he was so disturbed in his mind that he was on the point of going away without marking the package, when, looking over his shoulder, he suddenly caught sight of the Cockalorum standing close beside him, carefully holding an inkstand, with a pen in it, in one of his claws.

"Oh! thank you very much," said Davy, taking the pen and dipping it in the ink. "And will you please tell me his name?"

The Cockalorum, who still had his head done up in flannel, and was looking rather ill, paused for a moment to reflect, and then murmured, "Mark him '*Confectionery.*'"

This struck Davy as being a very happy idea, and he accordingly printed "CON-FEXIONRY" on the package in his very best manner. The Cockalorum, with his head turned critically on one side, carefully inspected the marking, and then, after earnestly gazing for a moment at the inkstand, gravely drank the rest of the ink and offered the empty inkstand to Davy.

"I don't want it, thank you," said Davy, stepping back.

"No more do I," murmured the Cockalorum, and, tossing the inkstand into the sea, flew away in his usual clumsy fashion.

Davy, after a last mournful look at the package of brown sugar, turned away, and was setting off along the beach again, when he heard a gurgling sound coming from behind a great hummock of sand, and, peeping cautiously around one end of it, he was startled at seeing an enormous whale lying stretched out on the sand basking in the sun, and lazily fanning himself with the flukes of his tail. The great creature had on a huge white garment, buttoned up in front, with a lot of live seals flopping and wriggling at one of the button-holes, and with a great chain cable leading from them to a pocket at one side. Before Davy could retreat the Whale caught sight of him and called out, in a tremendous voice, "How d'ye do, Bub?"

"I'm pretty well, I thank you," said Davy, with his usual politeness to man and beast. "How are you, sir?"

"Hearty!" thundered the Whale; "never felt better in all my life. But it's rather warm lying here in the sun."

"Why don't you take off your"—here Davy stopped, not knowing exactly what it was the Whale had on.

"Waistcoat," said the Whale, condescendingly. "It's a canvas-back-duck waistcoat. The front of it is made of wild duck, you see, and the back of it out of the foretop-sail of a brig. I've heard they always have watches on board of ships, but I couldn't find any on this one, so I had to satisfy myself with a bit of chain cable by way of a watch-guard. I think this bunch of seals rather sets it off, don't you?"

"Yes, rather," said Davy doubtfully; "only they slobber so."

"Ah, reminds me that it's wash-day," said the Whale; and here he spouted a great stream of water out of the top of his head and let it run down in a little cascade all over the front of his waistcoat. The seals seemed to enjoy this amazingly, and flopped about in an ecstacy.

"What do whales eat?" said Davy, who thought it was a good time for picking up a little information.

"Warious whales wants warious wiands," replied the Whale. "That's an old sea-saw, you know. For my part I'm particularly fond of small buoys."

"I don't think that is a very nice taste," said Davy, beginning to feel very uneasy.

"Oh! don't be frightened," bellowed the Whale, good naturedly. "I don't mean live boys. I mean the little red things that float about in the water. Some of 'em have lights on 'em, and *them* are particularly nice and crisp."

"Is it nice being a Whale?" said Davy, who was anxious to change the subject.

"Famous!" said the Whale, with an affable roar. "Great fun, I assure you! We have fish-balls every night, you know."

"Fish-balls at night!" exclaimed Davy. "Why we always have ours for breakfast."

"Nonsense!" thundered the Whale, with a laugh that made the beach quake; "I don't mean anything to eat. I mean dancing parties."

"And do *you* dance?" said Davy, thinking that if he did it must be a very extraordinary performance.

"Dance?" said the Whale, with a reverberating chuckle. "Bless you! I'm as nimble as a sixpence. By the way I'll show you the advantage of having a bit of whalebone in one's composition;" and with these words the Whale curled himself up, then flattened out suddenly with a tremendous flop, and, shooting through the air like a flying elephant, disappeared with a great splash in the sea.

Davy stood anxiously watching the spot where he went down, in the hope that he would come up again; but he soon discovered that the Whale had gone for good. The seas was violently tossed about for a few moments, and then began circling out into great rings around the spot where the Whale had gone down. These soon disappeared, however, and the water resumed its lazy ebb and flow upon the shore; and Davy, feeling quite lonesome and deserted, sat down on the sand, and gazed mournfully out upon the sea.

• CHAPTER XIII •

THE TALKING WAVES,
AND THE OLD SEA-DOG

I wonder why the ocean doesn't keep still sometimes, and not be moving its edge about all the time," said Davy, after watching the waves that constantly rolled up on the beach and then rolled back again, looking like creamy soap-suds.

"That couldn't do at all!" said a Wave that rolled almost up to his feet. "The beach gets mussed, you see, and we have to smooth it off again. The sea is always tidy;" and there the Wave broke with a little, murmuring laugh, and rolled back again, all in a foam.

Davy was so astonished that it almost took away his breath. A talking Wave was certainly the most marvelous thing he had met with, and in an instant he was lying flat on his face, trembling with eagerness, and waiting for the next Wave to roll up on the shore.

It came in a moment, and gently whispered, "If we didn't wet the sand once in a while there wouldn't be any nuts on the beach-trees,—no nuts on the trees, and no shells on the shore;" and here this Wave broke in its turn into foam, and ran back into the sea.

"This is perfectly delicious!" said Davy, joyfully, and as the next Wave rolled up to him he softly asked, "Do you know the Whale?"

"Know him!" cried the Wave, passionately; "I should think I did! Many a time I've been spanked by his horrid old tail. The nasty, blundering, floundering, walloping old"— and here the end of the sentence dribbled way in a sort of washy whisper.

"Such a mouth!" said the next Wave, taking up the story. "Like a fishing-smack lined with red morocco! And such a temper! I wouldn't be so crusty for all"—but just here the Wave toppled over as usual, and the rest of the sentence ran back into the sea.

"Once," said the next Wave, still scolding about the Whale, — "once he got so far up on the shore that he couldn't get back into the water for a long time, and he blamed me for it, and called me names. He said I was a mean, low tide;" but just as Davy was eagerly listening for the rest of the story this Wave, like the rest, broke into foam and washed away.

"It's really too ridiculous, the way they break off their sentences!" cried Davy, impatiently.

"Is it, indeed!" said a big Wave, coming in with a rush. "Perhaps you'd like to get acquainted with an angry sea!"

It was an angry sea, indeed; for, as the Wave said this, the ocean was suddenly lashed into fury, the water rose into huge, green billows that came tossing up on the shore, and Davy, scrambling to his feet, ran for his life. The air was filled with flying spray, and he could hear the roar of the water coming on behind him with a mighty rush as he ran across the beach, not daring to stop until he found himself out of reach of the angry ocean, on a high bluff of sand. Here he stopped, quite out of breath, and looked back.

The wind was blowing fiercely, and a cloud of spray was dashed in his face as he turned toward it, and presently the air was filled with lobsters, eels, and wriggling fishes that were being carried inshore by the gale. Suddenly, to Davy's astonishment, a dog came sailing along. He was being helplessly blown about among the lobsters, uneasily jerking his tail from side to side to keep it out of reach of their great claws, and giving short nervous barks from time to time, as though he were firing signal-guns of distress. In fact, he seemed to be having such a hard time of it that Davy caught him by the ear as he was going by, and landed him in safety on the beach. He proved to be a very shaggy, battered-looking animal, in an old pea-jacket, with a weather-beaten tarpaulin hat jammed on the side of his head, and a patch over one eye; altogether he was the most extraordinary-looking animal that could be imagined, and Davy stood staring at him, and wondering what sort of a dog he was.

"Are you a pointer?" he said at last, by way of opening conversation.

"Not I," said the Dog sulkily. "It's rude to point. I'm an old Sea-Dog, come ashore in a gale."

Here he stared doubtfully at Davy for a moment, and then said in a husky voice—

"What's the difference between a dog-watch and a watch-dog? It's a conundrum."

"I don't know," said Davy, who would have laughed if he had not been a little afraid of the Dog.

"A dog-watch keeps a watching on a bark," said the old Sea-Dog; "and a watch-dog keeps a barking on a watch." Here he winked at Davy, and said, "What's *your* name?" as if he had just mentioned his own.

"Davy"—began the little boy, but before he could say another word the old Sea-Dog growled, "Right you are!" and, handing him a folded paper, trotted gravely away, swaggering, as he went, like a seafaring man.

The paper was addressed to "*Davy Jones*," and was headed inside, "*Binnacle Bob: His werses;*" and below these words Davy found the following story:—

To inactivity inclined
Was Captain Parker Pitch's mind;
In point of fact, 'twas fitted for
A sedentary life ashore.

His disposition, so to speak,
Was nautically soft and weak;
He feared the rolling ocean, and
He very much preferred the land.

A stronger-minded man by far
Was gallant Captain Thompson Tar;
And (what was very wrong, I think)
He marked himself with India ink.

He boldly sailed the "Soaking Sue"
When angry gales and tempests blew,
And even from the nor-nor-east
He didn't mind 'em in the least.

Now, Captain Parker Pitch's sloop
Was called the "Cozy Chickencoop,"—
A truly comfortable craft,
With ample state-rooms fore and aft.

No foolish customs of the deep,
Like "watches," robbed his crew of sleep;
That estimable lot of men
Were all in bed at half-past ten.

At seven bells, one stormy day,
Bold Captain Tar came by that way,
And in a voice extremely coarse
He roared "Ahoy!" till he was hoarse.

Next morning, of his own accord,
This able seaman came aboard,
And made the following remark
Concerning Captain Pitch's bark:—

"Avast!" says he, "Belay! What cheer!
How comes this little wessel here?
Come, tumble up your crew," says he,
"And navigate a bit with me!"

Says captain Pitch, "I can't refuse
To join you on a friendly cruise;
But you'll oblige me, Captain Tar,
By not a-taking of me far."

At this reply from Captain Pitch,
Bold Thompson gave himself a hitch;
It cut him to the heart to find
A seaman in this frame of mind.

"Avast!" says he; "we'll bear away
For Madagascar and Bombay,
Then down the coast to Yucatan,
Kamtschatka, Guinea, and Japan.

"Stand off for Egypt, Turkey, Spain,
Australia, and the Spanish Main,
Then through the nor-west passage for
Van Dieman's Land and Labrador."

Says Captain Pitch, "The ocean swell
Makes me exceedingly unwell,
And, Captain Tar, before we start,
Pray join me in a friendly tart."

And shall I go and take and hide
The sneaking trick that Parker tried?
Oh! no. I very much prefer
To state his actions as they were:

With marmalade he first began
To tempt that bluff seafaring man,
Then fed him all the afternoon
With custard in a table-spoon.

No mariner, however tough,
Can thrive upon this kind of stuff;
And Thompson soon appeared to be
A feeble-minded child of three.

He cried for cakes and lollipops;
He played with dolls and humming-tops;
He even ceased to roar "I'm blowed!"
And shook a rattle, laughed, and crowed.

When Parker saw the seamen gaze
Upon the captain's cunning ways,
Base envy thrilled him through and through,
And he became a child of two.

Now, Parker had in his employ
A mate, two seamen, and a boy,
The mate was fond as he could be
Of babies, and he says, says he, —

"Why, messmates, as we're all agreed
Sea-bathing is the thing we need,
Let's drop these hinfants off the quarter!"
(They did, in fourteen fathom water).

—and here the story became abruptly to an end.

Davy was quite distressed at this, particularly as the dreadful thought came to his mind that some babies do not know how to swim, and he was therefore very well satisfied when he saw that the old Sea-Dog had apparently changed his mind about going away, and was swaggering along toward him again.

"If you please," said Davy, as the surly creature came within hearing distance, — "if you please, sir, were the two little captains drowned?"

"Well, sticking, as it were, to the truth, they were not," replied the old Sea-Dog, very gruffly.

"Then, why don't you say so in the story?" said Davy.

Now, this was pretty bold of him, for old Sea-Dogs don't much like to have fault found with their verses, and this particular old Sea-Dog evidently did not like it at all, for, after staring at Davy for a moment, he began walking slowly around him in such a threatening manner that Davy, thinking that perhaps he meant to jump on him from behind, began also turning so as to keep his face always toward the Dog. Meanwhile, as you may well believe, he began to feel very sorry that he had said anything about the verses.

Presently the old Sea-Dog broke into a clumsy canter, like a weary old circus horse, and as he went heavily around the circle he began to explain about the story. "You see there's more of it," said he, wheezing dreadfully as he galloped; "but then I haven't had the time to put the rest of it in rhyme. It's all about old Thompson's crew as stayed aboard the 'Soaking Sue,' and saw the skippers floating by and hauled 'em out and got 'em dry, and when the little creeturs cried they gave 'em something warm inside, and being as they had no bed they stowed 'em in a bunk instead,"—but just at this moment the old Sea-Dog, who had been constantly increasing his speed, disappeared in a most extraordinary manner in a whirling cloud of sand, and Davy, who was by this time spinning around like a teetotum, discovered that he himself was rapidly boring his way, like a big screw, down into the beach. This was, of course, a very alarming state of things; but, before Davy could make an effort to free himself, the whirling cloud of sand burst upon him with a loud, roaring sound like the sea, and he felt himself going directly down through the beach, with the sand pouring in upon him as if he had been inside of a huge hour-glass. He had just time to notice that, instead of scraping him, the sand had a delightful ticklesome feeling about it, when he went completely through the beach, and landed, with a gentle thump, flat on his back, with tall grass waving about him.

CHAPTER XIV

THE END OF THE BELIEVING VOYAGE

hen Davy sat up and looked around him he found himself in a beautiful meadow, with the sun shining brightly on the grass and the wild flowers. The air was filled with dainty-colored insects, darting about in the warm sunshine, and chirping cheerily as they flew, and at a little distance the Goblin was sitting on the grass, attentively examining a great, struggling creature that he was holding down by its wings.

"I suppose," said the Goblin, as if Davy's sudden appearance was the most ordinary thing in the world,—"I suppose that this is about the funniest bug that flies."

"What is it?" said Davy, cautiously edging away.

"It's a Cricket-Bat," said the Goblin, rapping familiarly with his knuckles on its hard shell. "His body is like a boot-jack, and his wings are like a pair of umbrellas,"

"But, you know, a Cricket-Bat is something to play with!" said Davy, surprised at the Goblin's ignorance.

"Well, *you* may play with it if you like. *I* don't want to," said the Goblin, carelessly tossing the great creature over to Davy, and walking away.

The Cricket-Bat made a swoop at Davy, knocking him over like a feather, and then, with a loud snort, flew away across the meadow. It dashed here and there at flying things of every kind, and, turning on its side, knocked them, one after another, quite out of sight, until, to Davy's delight, the Cockalorum came into view, flying across the meadow in his usual blundering fashion. At sight of him the Cricket-Bat gave another triumphant snort, and with a wild plunge at the great creature knocked him floundering into the tall grass, and with a loud, whirring sound disappeared in a distant wood.

Davy ran to the spot where the Cockalorum had fallen, and found him sitting helplessly in the grass, looking dreadfully rumpled, and staring confusedly, as if wondering what had happened to him. As Davy came running up he murmured, in a reproachful way, "Oh! it's you is it? Well, then, I don't want any more of it."

"Upon my word I didn't do it," cried Davy, trying to keep from laughing. "It was the Cricket-Bat."

"And what did *he* want?" murmured the Cockalorum, very sadly.

"Oh! he was only having a game of cricket with you," said Davy soothingly. "You were the ball, you know."

The Cockalorum pondered over this for a moment, and then murmuring, "I prefer croquet," floundered away through the waving grass. Davy, who for once felt sorry for the ridiculous old creature, was just setting off after him, when a voice cried, "Come on! Come on!" and Davy, looking across the meadow, saw the Goblin beckoning vigorously to him, apparently in great excitement.

"What's the matter?" cried Davy, pushing his way through the thick grass.

"Oh, my! oh, my!" shrieked the Goblin, who was almost bursting with laughter. "Here's that literary hack again!"

Davy peered through a clump of bushes, and discovered a large red animal, with white spots on its sides, clumsily rummaging about in the tall grass and weeds. Its appearance was so formidable that he was just about whispering to the Goblin, "Let's run!" when the monster raised its head, and, after gazing about for an instant, gave a loud, triumphant whistle.

"Why, it's Ribsy!" cried Davy, running forward. "It's Ribsy, only he's grown enormously fat."

It was Ribsy, indeed, eating with all his might, and with his skin so stretched by his extreme fatness that the hair stood straight up all over it like a brush. The name on his side was twisted about beyond all hope of making it out, and his collar had quite disappeared in a deep crease about his neck. In fact, his whole appearance was so alarming that Davy anxiously inquired of him what he had been eating.

"Everything!" said Ribsy, enthusiastically,—"grass, nuts, bugs, birds, and berries! All of 'em taste good. I could eat both of you easily," he added, glaring hungrily down upon Davy and the Goblin.

"Try that fellow first," said the Goblin, pointing to a large, round insect that went flying by, humming like a top. Ribsy snapped at it, and swallowed it, and the next instant disappeared with a tremendous explosion in the a great cloud of smoke.

"What was that?" said Davy, in a terrified whisper.

"A Hum Bug," said the Goblin calmly. "When a cab-horse on a vacation talks about eating you, a Hum Bug is a pretty good thing to take the conceit out of him. They're loaded, you see, and they go booming along as innocently as you please; but if you touch 'em—why, 'There you aren't!' as the Hole-keeper says."

"The Hole-keeper isn't himself any more," said Davy, mournfully.

"Not altogether himself, but somewhat," said a voice; and Davy, looking around, was astonished to find the Hole-keeper standing beside him. He was a most extraordinary-looking object, being nothing but Davy's parcel marked, "CONFEXIONRY," with arms and legs and a head to it. At the sight of him the Goblin fell flat on his back, and covered his face with his hands.

"I'm quite aware that my appearance is not prepossessing," said the Hole-keeper, with a scornful look at the Goblin. "In fact, I'm nothing but a quarter of a pound of 'plain,' and the price isn't worth mentioning."

"But how did you *ever* come to be alive again, at all?" said Davy.

"Well," said the Hole-keeper, "the truth of the matter is, that after you went away the Cockalorum fell into reading the *Vacuum;* and, if you'll believe it, there wasn't a word in it about my going back into the raw material."

"I *do* believe that," said Davy; but the Hole-keeper, without noticing the interruption, went on:—

"*Then,* of course, I got up and came away. Meanwhile the Cockalorum is gorging himself with information."

"I saw him just now," said Davy, laughing, "and he didn't act as if he had learned anything very lately. I don't think he'll find much in your book;" and here he went off into another fit of laughter.

"Ah! but just think of the lots and lots of things he *won't* find," exclaimed the Hole-keeper. "Everything he doesn't find in it is something worth knowing. By the way, your friend seems to have having some sort of fit. Give him some dubbygrums;" and with this the Hole-keeper stalked pompously away.

"The smell of sugar always gives me the craw-craws," said the Goblin, in a stifled voice, rolling on the ground and keeping his hands over his face. "Get me some water."

"I haven't anything to get it in," said Davy, helplessly.

"There's a buttercup behind you," groaned the Goblin, and Davy, turning, saw a buttercup growing on a stem almost as tall as he was himself. He picked it, and hurried away across the meadow to look for water, the buttercup, meanwhile, growing in his hand in a surprising manner, until it became a full-sized teacup, with a handle conveniently growing on one side. Davy, however, had become so accustomed to this sort of thing that he would not have been greatly surprised if a saucer had also made its appearance.

Presently he came upon a sparkling little spring, gently bubbling up in a marshy place, with high, sedgy grass growing about it, and being a very neat little boy he took off his shoes and stockings, and carefully picked his way over the oozy ground to the edge of the spring itself. He was just bending over to dip the cup into the spring, when the ground under his feet began trembling like jelly, and then, giving itself a convulsive shake, threw him head-foremost into the water.

For a moment Davy had a very curious sensation, as though his head and his arms and his legs were all trying to get inside of his jacket, and then he came sputtering to the top of the water and scrambled ashore. To his astonishment he saw that the spring had spread itself out into a little lake, and that the sedge-grass had grown to an enormous height, and was waving far above his head. Then he was startled by a tremendous roar of laughter, and looking around he saw the Goblin, who was now apparently at least twenty feet high, standing beside the spring.

"Oh, lor! Oh, lor!" cried the Goblin, in an uncontrollable fit of merriment. "Another minute and you wouldn't have been bigger than a peanut!"

"What's the matter with me?" said Davy, not knowing what to make of it all.

"Matter?" cried the Goblin. "Why, you've been and gone and fallen into an Elastic Spring, that's all. If you'd got in at stretch tide, early in the morning, you'd have been a perfect giraffe; but you got in at shrink tide and—oh, my! oh, my!" and here he went off into another fit of laughter.

"I don't think it's anything to laugh at," cried Davy, with the tears starting to his eyes, "and I'm sure I don't know what I'm going to do."

"Oh! don't worry," said the Goblin, good-naturedly. "I'll take a dip myself, just to be companionable, and tomorrow morning we can get back to any size you like."

"I wish you'd take these things in with you," said Davy pointing to his shoes and stockings. "They're big enough for Badorful."

All right!" cried the Goblin. "Here we go;" and, taking the shoes and stockings in his hand, he plunged into the spring, and a moment afterward scrambled out exactly Davy's size.

"Now, that's what I call a nice, tidy size," said the Goblin complacently, while Davy was squeezing his feet into his wet shoes. "What do you say to a ride on a field-mouse?"

"That will be glorious!" said Davy.

"Well, there goes the sun," said the Goblin; "it will be moonlight presently, and moonlight is the time for mouse-back riding;" and as he spoke, the sun went down with a boom like a distant gun, and left them in the dark. The next moment the moon rose above the trees and beamed down pleasantly upon them, and the Goblin, taking Davy by the hand, led him into the wood.

"Freckles," said the Goblin, "what time is it?"

They were now in the densest part of the wood, where the moon was shining brightly on a little pool with rushes growing about it, and the Goblin was speaking to a large Toad.

"Forty croaks," said the Toad, in a husky whisper; and then, as a frog croaked in the pool, he added, "That makes it forty-one. The Snoopers have come in, and Thimbletoes is shaking in his boots." And with these words the Toad coughed, and then hopped heavily away.

"What does he mean?" whispered Davy.

"He means that the fairies are here, and *that* means that we won't get our ride," said the Goblin, rather sulkily.

"And who is Thimbletoes?" said Davy.

"He's the Prime Minister," said the Goblin. "You see, if any one of the Snoopers finds out something the Queen didn't know before, out goes the Prime Minister, and the Snooper pops into his boots. Thimbletoes doesn't fancy that, you know, because the Prime Minister has all the honey he wants, by way of a salary. Now, here's the mouse-stable, and don't you speak a word—mind!"

As the Goblin said this they came upon a little, thatched building, about the size of a baby-house, standing just beyond the pool; and the Goblin, cautiously pushing open the door, stole noiselessly in, with Davy following at his heels, trembling with excitement.

The little building was curiously lighted up by a vast number of fire-flies, hung from the ceiling by loops of cobweb; and Davy could see several spiders hurrying about among them, stirring them up when the light grew dim. The field-mice were stabled in little stalls on either side, each one with his tail neatly tied in a bow-knot to a ring at one side; and, at the farther end of the stable was a buzzing throng of fairies, with their shining clothes and gauzy wings sparkling beautifully in the soft light. Just beyond them Davy saw the Queen sitting on a raised throne, with a little mullen-stalk for a sceptre, and beside her was the Prime Minister, in a terrible state of agitation.

"Now, here's this Bandybug," the Prime Minister was saying. "What does *he* know about untying the knots of a cord of wood?"

"Nothing!" said the Queen, positively. "Absolutely nothing!"

"And then," continued the Prime Minister, "the idea of his presuming to tell your Gossamer Majesty that he can hear the bark of the dogwood trees"—

"Bosh!" cried the Queen. "Paint him with raspberry jam, and put him to bed in a bee-hive. That'll make him smart, at all events."

Here the Prime Minister began dancing about in an ecstasy, until the Queen knocked him over with the mullen-stalk, and shouted, "Silence! and plenty of it, too. Bring in Berrylegs."

Berrylegs, who proved to be a wiry little Fairy, with a silver coat and tight, cherry-colored trousers, was immediately brought in. His little wings fairly bristled with defiance, and his manner, as he stood before the Queen, was so impudent, that Davy felt morally certain there was going to be a scene.

"May it please your Transparent Highness,"—began Berrylegs.

"Skip all that!" interrupted the Queen, flourishing her mullen-stalk.

"Skip, yourself!" said Berrylegs, boldly in reply. "Don't you suppose I know how to talk to a Queen?"

The Queen turned very pale, and, after a hurried consultation with the Prime Minister, said faintly, "Have it your own way;" and Berrylegs began again.

"May it please your transparent Highness, I've found out how the needles get into the haystacks."

As Berrylegs said this a terrible commotion arose at once among the fairies. The Prime Minister cried out, "Oh, come, I say! That's not fair, you know," and the Queen became so agitated that she began taking great bites off the end of the mullen-stalk in a dazed sort of way; and Davy noticed that the Goblin, in his excitement, was trying to climb up on one of the mouse-stalls, so as to get a better view of what was going on. At last the Queen, whose mouth was now quite filled with bits of the mullen-stalk, mumbled, "Get to the point."

"It ought to be a sharp one, being about needles," said the Prime Minister, attempting a joke, with a feeble laugh, but no one paid the slightest attention to him; and Berrylegs, who was now positively swelling with importance, called out, in a loud voice, "It comes from using sewing-machines when they sow the hay-seed!"

The Prime Minister gave a shriek, and fell flat on his face, and the Queen began jumping frantically up and down, and beating about on all sides of her with the end of the mullen-stalk, when suddenly a large Cat walked into the stable, and the fairies fled in all directions. There was no mistaking the Cat, and Davy, forgetting entirely the Goblin's caution, exclaimed, "Why! it's Solomon!"

The next instant the lights disappeared, and Davy found himself in total darkness, with Solomon's eyes shining at him like two balls of fire. There was a confused sound of sobs and cries and the squeaking of mice, among which could be heard the Goblin's voice, crying, "Davy! Davy!" in a reproachful way; then the eyes disappeared, and a moment afterward the stable was lifted off the ground and violently shaken.

"That's Solomon, trying to get at the mice," thought Davy. "I wish the old thing had stayed away," he added aloud, and as he said this the little stable was broken all to bits, and he found himself sitting on the ground in the forest.

The moon had disappeared, and snow was falling rapidly, and the sound of the distant chimes reminded Davy that it must be past midnight, and that Christmas-day had come. Solomon's eyes were shining in the darkness like a pair of coach-lamps, and, as Davy sat looking at them, a ruddy light began to glow between them, and presently the figure of the Goblin appeared, dressed in scarlet, as when he had first come. The reddish light was shining through his stomach again, as though the coals had been fanned into life once more, and as Davy gazed at him it grew brighter and stronger, and finally burst into blaze. Then Solomon's eyes gradually took the form of great brass balls, and presently the figure of the long-lost Colonel came into view just above them, affectionately hugging his clock. He was gazing mournfully down upon the poor Goblin, who was now blazing like a dry chip, and as the light of the fire grew brighter and stronger the trees about slowly took the shape of an old-fashioned fireplace with a high mantel-shelf above it, and then Davy found himself curled up in the big easy-chair, with his

dear old grandmother bending over him, and saying gently, "Davy! Davy! Come and have some dinner, my dear!"

In fact, the Believing Voyage was ended.

ABOUT THE ILLUSTRATOR

Greg Hildebrandt was born in Detroit, Michigan in 1939. Interested early in animation and special effects, he and his twin brother began their careers in animated and documentary films. In 1970, they moved into commercial and book illustration. Influenced heavily by N.C. Wyeth, Howard Pyle, and Maxfield Parrish, Greg and his brother quickly became successful illustrators, and completed many mass-market and juvenile illustrated books. Proof of their success came in 1976 when they received the coveted Gold Medal from the Society of Illustrators. Greg and his brother then went on to illustrate three phenomenally successful J.R.R. Tolkien Calendars, the famous "Star Wars" poster, and wrote and illustrated their first best-selling novel, *Urshurak*. In 1983, Greg began his solo career illustrating the classics. After completing *A Christmas Carol* and *Greg Hildebrandt's Favorite Fairy Tales* for Simon and Schuster, Greg began illustrating for this Unicorn line of classics and quality juvenile. So long as there are fairy tales and classics which warm the hearts of children of all ages, Greg Hildebrandt's brush will never be silent.